The
SPRITE
SISTERS

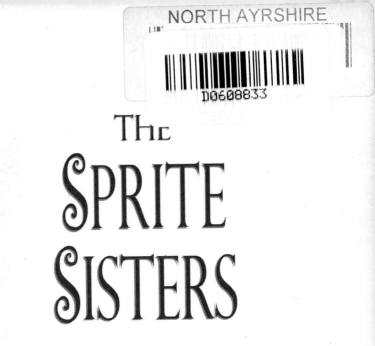

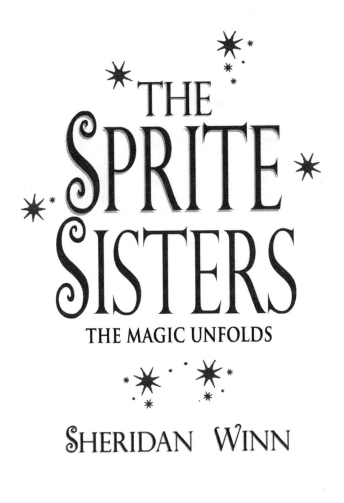

THE SPRITE SISTERS

THE MAGIC UNFOLDS

SHERIDAN WINN

PICCADILLY PRESS • LONDON

First published in Great Britain in 2008
by Piccadilly Press Ltd,
5 Castle Road, London NW1 8PR
www.piccadillypress.co.uk

A catalogue record for this book is available
from the British Library.

ISBN: 978 1 85340 991 2

Printed and bound in Great Britain by CPI Bookmarque, CR0 4TD
Cover design by Simon Davis
Cover illustration by Anna Gould
Sprite Towers map by Chris Winn

Mixed Sources
Product group from well-managed
forests and other controlled sources
www.fsc.org   Cert no. TT-COC-002227
FSC   © 1996 Forest Stewardship Council

For my sister Mellie
and my cousin Lizzie,
who remember the
'grasshopper' summer

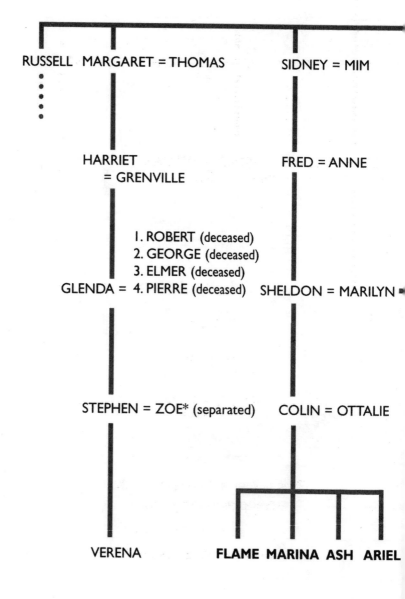

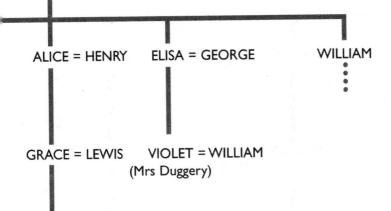

ARTHUR SPRITE = LILY PYE

ALICE = HENRY   ELISA = GEORGE   WILLIAM

GRACE = LEWIS   VIOLET = WILLIAM
(Mrs Duggery)

THE
SPRITE
FAMILY

This is just a small part of the
complete family tree.

* Zoe is the sister of Oswald Foffington-Plinker

THE CIRCLE OF POWER

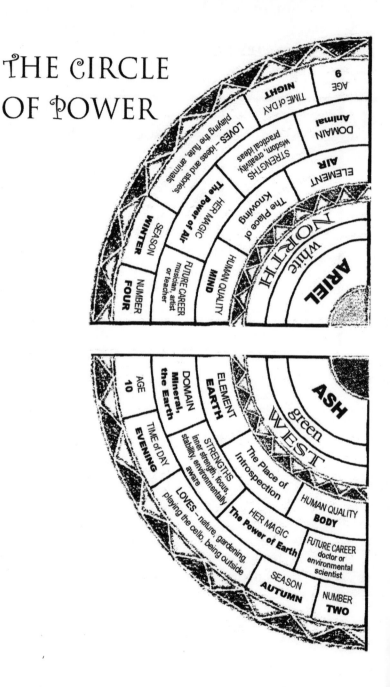

ARIEL

white

NORTH

ELEMENT
AIR

The Place of Knowing

STRENGTHS
wisdom, creativity,
practical ideas

LOVES – ideas and stories,
playing the flute, animals

The Power of Air

HER MAGIC

FUTURE CAREER
musician, artist
or teacher

HUMAN QUALITY
MIND

SEASON
WINTER

NUMBER
FOUR

AGE
6

TIME of DAY
NIGHT

DOMAIN
Animal

ASH

green

WEST

ELEMENT
EARTH

DOMAIN
Mineral,
the Earth

STRENGTHS
inner strength, focus,
stability, environmentally
aware

The Place of Introspection

HER MAGIC
The Power of Earth

LOVES – nature, gardening,
playing the cello, being outside

HUMAN QUALITY
BODY

FUTURE CAREER
doctor or
environmental
scientist

SEASON
AUTUMN

NUMBER
TWO

TIME of DAY
EVENING

AGE
10

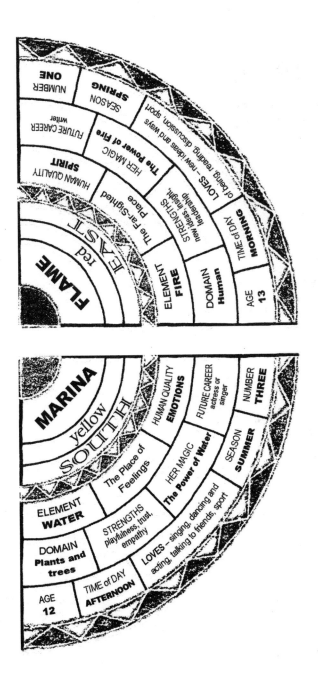

FLAME
red **EAST**

NUMBER	ONE
SEASON	SPRING
FUTURE CAREER	writer
HER MAGIC	The Power of Fire
HUMAN QUALITY	SPIRIT
The Far-Sighted Place
STRENGTHS	new ideas, insight, leadership
LOVES	new ideas and ways of being, reading, discussion, sport
ELEMENT	FIRE
DOMAIN	Human
TIME of DAY	MORNING
AGE	13

MARINA
yellow **SOUTH**

HUMAN QUALITY	EMOTIONS
FUTURE CAREER	actress or singer
NUMBER	THREE
SEASON	SUMMER
The Place of Feelings
HER MAGIC	The Power of Water
ELEMENT	WATER
STRENGTHS	playfulness, trust, empathy
DOMAIN	Plants and trees
LOVES	singing, dancing and acting, talking to friends, sport
TIME of DAY	AFTERNOON
AGE	12

CHAPTER ONE

WARNING SIGNS

FLAME SPRITE felt it like a shiver. An icy shiver that started in her left ear and ran all the way down her spine, so suddenly, so unexpectedly, that she caught her breath and stopped in her tracks.

She shuddered in the bright June sunshine. It's a warning, she thought. She had just rounded the corner of the Quad in front of Drysdale's School on Monday morning, on her way to assembly. Now she stood stock-still, unable to move.

A second icy wave, like an echo, made her shiver again.

What is it, she wondered, gazing at the tarmac for a moment.

She lifted her gaze upwards – and drew a sharp intake of breath. Less than ten metres away, a large silver car glided past her towards the exit. The driver, an elegant woman with a chignon of pale blond hair, gave her a hard stare.

Glenda Glass: the Sprite Sisters' sworn enemy. The woman who had tried to hurt them nine days ago at the school concert – and nearly succeeded.

Shaken as she was, Flame met the woman's stare with a level gaze. She felt her jaw tighten as she noticed Glenda Glass's cold, rather eerie smile.

Glenda is trying to threaten me, thought Flame. Even though she was hurt by her own magic when our Circle of Power protected us, she's not going to give up – I can feel it.

Flame held her head high, pulled back her shoulders and stood tall.

You will not hurt us, she thought, staring at the receding car. You will not destroy our magic. You can try, but you will not win . . .

As she turned, she saw Verena Glass walking over the Quad towards the school hall.

The icy shiver passed down her back a third time, as Flame looked at the tall, blond-haired girl.

This feeling of foreboding is something to do with *her*, she thought. We must be careful about Verena, as well as Glenda. We must be very, very careful . . .

With a sudden start, Flame was brought back to the 'real' world, as Marina bashed her playfully on the back.

'Come on, Flame!' she said. 'We've got to get to assembly! Concert result, remember?'

Then, seeing her older sister's pale face, Marina stopped. 'You okay?'

'Yep,' said Flame, with a small smile. 'Let's go.'

I don't want to alarm my sisters today, she thought. I'll wait and see what this feeling is about, first.

Twenty minutes later, the pupils and teachers of Drysdale's School sat in the huge hall, with its high ceiling and dark wood-panelled walls. The school had stood to sing two rousing hymns. They had listened to the chaplain's words. Now, they sat eagerly awaiting the results of the National Schools Music Competition.

Nine days earlier, the Sprite Sisters had performed with other members of the school. If Drysdale's won the regional heat, its musicians would play in the finals at the Royal Albert Hall in London, competing against two other schools.

Everyone sat up, alert, as Batty Blenkinsop, headmaster of Drysdale's, walked towards the microphone with his long, lolloping stride.

Flame, Marina, Ash and Ariel Sprite held their breath. Would Drysdale's win?

'And, now,' announced Batty Blenkinsop. 'The result of

the National Schools Music Competition . . .'

There was absolute silence. Everybody waited.

Batty coughed.

'*Come on!*' the pupils whispered.

'We have all been waiting to hear . . .' said Batty, clearing his throat.

More silence. Batty cleared his throat again. Several pupils groaned with impatience.

Batty Blenkinsop looked out at the school. Then, suddenly, he gave a big smile and announced, '*We won!*'

A loud hurrah went up.

'Drysdale's will be one of the three finalist schools playing at the Royal Albert Hall on Saturday evening!' Batty said proudly. 'Well done, all the musicians and singers who took part – and the very best of luck to you on Saturday!'

There was a loud cheer from the whole school and everybody clapped their hands.

'Fantastic!' said Flame to her friend, Pia, sitting beside her.

'Well done, Flame!' said Pia, smiling at her. Doe-eyed Pia was small and graceful like a deer, whereas Flame was tall and strong. 'You deserve it,' she added.

Flame turned in her seat to see Marina smiling at her a few rows behind. They both knew what this meant for the Sprite Sisters.

We *do* deserve it, thought Flame, looking round to see if she could spot Ash and Ariel. Only the Sprite Sisters and their grandmother knew what had really happened at the concert and what they had achieved. Not only had they had to play their very best to an audience of five hundred people, but they also had to use their magic powers to repel an attack of magic from Glenda Glass.

This vengeful woman was determined to harm the Sprite Sisters, as a way of getting at Grandma. Glenda had never forgiven Marilyn Sprite for being a better ballerina than her, when they danced in the same *corps de ballet* forty-five years ago – or for marrying Sheldon Sprite, the owner of Sprite Towers.

A Sprite herself, Glenda came from the line in the family that had broken the Sprite Code of Honour, which decreed that magic power must only be used for good. This branch had 'gone bad' and used its magic powers against other people. Fuelled by jealousy and anger, Glenda's dark power had grown stronger over the years.

Marilyn Sprite's power, by contrast, had weakened since Glenda attacked her forty-five years ago. She used her magic to defend herself that terrible night, and in desperation wished Glenda dead. Since then – perhaps because she was a 'good' Sprite who used her magic to hurt someone – her powers had disappeared. Although she had lost her power, her four granddaughters had inherited the magic that ran through the family. This power had been in the family for hundreds of years, but few Sprites had it. Dad, for instance, did not have it, though his mother had.

5

Two weeks ago, on her ninth birthday, Ariel had come into her powers. Each of her three older sisters had had the same experience on their ninth birthdays. Now Ariel had completed the circle, for each of the sisters' powers related to one of the four directions on the compass.

Intense, spirited Flame stood at the East of the compass. Her power was the power of Fire. At the South of the compass, playful, caring Marina had the power of Water. Practical Ash, who stood strong like a tree and who was named after one, stood on the West of the compass and harnessed the power of Earth. And at the North of the compass stood Ariel; light-hearted but insightful, despite her young years, she brought the power of Air.

The Circle of Power was complete. Together the Sprite Sisters were balanced and powerful.

Now, they sat in the grand school hall thinking about their music – which they loved. They had worked hard to help Drysdale's School win the regional final of the competition, and had given a superb performance with their quartet.

For a moment, Flame Sprite wanted to cry. We did it, she thought, looking up at the high ceiling. A few rows behind, Marina watched as Flame lifted her face – saw her long copper-coloured hair tip down her back, knew her sister was holding back tears.

Flame is brave and strong and she sees ahead, thought

Marina. If Flame hadn't realised we should use the Circle of Power to protect ourselves from Glenda's dark magic, the concert would have been ruined and we could have been seriously hurt. It was Flame who realised that, by sitting on the stage in the positions of the four directions, we could make the blue light that would shield us from Glenda's magic – the Circle of Power. The magic we created was so strong that her dark magic bounced off it and hurtled back to her.

Marina swallowed hard. She loved and respected her elder sister – and she was thrilled that in a few days they would be playing their music in London.

I am so happy, she thought.

'Well done!' said her best friend, Janey McIver, beside her.

Marina laughed. 'Thanks, Janey!'

When assembly finished, the four Sprite Sisters rushed to find each other.

'We did it!' Flame, Marina and Ash shouted. 'We helped Drysdale's win the heat!'

'Fab-fantastic!' cried Ariel.

Flame looked down at her youngest sister's sweet face, with her big, grey eyes and ski-jump nose. 'Well done, pumpkin,' she said, stroking Ariel's soft blond hair.

Ariel beamed with pleasure. 'I'm so excited we're going to London!' she squeaked.

Ash, the quietest Sprite Sister, looked happy. Marina

gave her a hug, then playfully ruffled her short chestnut-brown hair.

'Get off!' laughed Ash, pushing her away.

Marina looked at Flame. 'We did it – we did it together!' she said, and the two older sisters gave each other a hug.

'Royal Albert Hall, here we come!' said Flame.

As the Sprite Sisters left the assembly hall, Flame stopped to talk to Mr Taylor, the music master. She did not see Verena Glass approach Marina, behind her, a few metres away.

'Hi – well done!' said Marina, smiling at Verena.

'Thank you,' she replied. 'And you!' Verena knew her soaring voice had helped Drysdale's to win the heat of the National Schools Music Competition. She had sung beautifully and was proud of the result.

Since Verena had spent Saturday afternoon at the rounders party at Sprite Towers, she had grown to like the Sprite Sisters, despite her wariness of Flame. She and Flame were matched too closely in intelligence and sporting ability to be anything other than competitive at school, and now that they liked the same boy – dark-eyed Quinn McIver – things were even more tricky.

However, Marina she felt comfortable with. An only child now living with her cold-hearted grandmother, Verena appreciated Marina's kind nature.

'Didn't we all do well!' said Marina. 'You are you

coming to London, aren't you?'

'Yes, of course,' smiled Verena. 'Amazing to be able to sing at the Royal Albert Hall! I'm not sure my grandmother will come though. She doesn't like London much – and she doesn't seem to care two hoots about my singing.'

'Oh, I'm sorry,' said Marina. She felt sad for Verena, but she was enormously relieved at the news that Glenda would not be at the London concert. 'How will you get there, then?' she asked.

'Well, I'll stay with my father, but I may need to get a lift with one of the other families going.'

'I'll ask Mum, if you like,' said Marina.

'Thanks – I'd appreciate that,' said Verena.

Just at that moment, Flame finished her conversation with Mr Taylor. She turned round, saw Marina talking to Verena – and the colour drained from her cheeks.

At the same time, Marina turned, saw Flame staring at her – her face as white as a sheet. She looked at her older sister with an expression that said, '*What?*'

Verena looked from one Sprite Sister to the other. They'd just won a place at the finals, and now Flame Sprite was staring at her with a look of dread.

What's the matter, wondered Verena. What does she think I've done?

Verena and Marina exchanged glances – and when they looked back at Flame, she had gone.

* * *

9

Back at Sprite Towers, Dad walked through to his home office, mug of coffee in hand. Some days he worked at his office in town, where his architectural practice was based, and some days he worked at home.

He hummed, as he often did when he was in a cheery mood. I wonder if Drysdale's has won a place at the finals, he thought, as he put the mug on his desk.

He sat down and for a few minutes sipped his coffee and thought about the week ahead. Then he noticed the letter from Oswald Foffington-Plinker, propped up on the top of the desk.

'Drat,' he muttered. For a moment, he wished he had gone straight into his town office and not seen the letter, but dealt with it must be. He had read it over a week ago and it had been sitting there ever since.

He sat back in his chair, opened the expensive white envelope and unfolded the letter.

There it was: Oswald Foffington-Plinker's expression of interest in purchasing Sprite Towers and its grounds.

Dad's heart sank, as it had done the first time he had read the letter. He scratched the back of his head and sighed.

The phone rang. He picked it up. 'Hello, Colin Sprite.'

'Morning, old chap, Oswald here.'

'Good morning, Oswald,' Dad replied in a measured voice.

'Just wanted a quick chat about my letter,' said Oswald

in a voice both oily and steely.

'I am just reading it again,' said Dad.

'Good, good,' said Oswald. 'Thought I'd give you some time to think about it. I wondered if we could arrange a visit for me and the other company directors to come and have a look round the place. Really believe the house would convert perfectly to a boutique hotel – spa, that sort of thing. There's so much space and potential – it's a perfect development site.'

Dad was silent. The thought of his family home in the hands of property developers filled him with despair. Then he said, 'Oswald, a visit is not necessary. We don't plan to sell Sprite Towers now or in the future.'

'Well, have a think about it, old chap,' said Oswald, undeterred. 'You know I couldn't help noticing last time I was there – some time ago now, of course – that the roof was in a bit of a state. Big old place to keep going, eh, especially when you've got four sets of school fees to find each term.'

Dad breathed out heavily. Oswald was right. The roof of Sprite Towers was not in good shape and his daughters' school fees were a constant pressure that would only increase as they got older.

Being the consummate salesman that he was, Oswald knew when to stop talking. 'Well, I'll let you get on. Come back to me when you've had a chance to *really* think it through with Ottalie. You're sitting on a goldmine, old chap.'

Dad put down the phone – and stared out of the window at the garden.

What should I do, he wondered. My architectural practice earns good money, but it will take a rich man to repair the roof of Sprite Towers. It's a big roof . . . My great-grandfather, Sidney Sprite, had made a fortune as a toffee manufacturer when he built Sprite Towers in 1910 and the roof probably hasn't been repaired since then . . . How will we pay for it all? We may have to take the girls out of Drysdale's . . . What's more important – a wonderful education for our daughters, or a wonderful home?

I'll take a closer look at the state of the roof this evening, he thought. Need to know exactly what we're dealing with.

Dad smiled as he remembered his father, Sheldon. He used to say, 'There must always be Sprites at Sprite Towers.' My father was a rich man, though, Dad thought. My mother would have been rich too, if the inheritance hadn't disappeared into thin air. There's no family money to fall back on now. If we're going to repair the roof of Sprite Towers, I will have to earn some serious cash – and *how* am I going to do that?

CHAPTER TWO

✳

GLENDA'S PLAN

✳

SUPPER AT Sprite Towers was a lively affair on Monday evening. Everyone was delighted about Drysdale's win and there was much to talk about. The Sprite Sisters were in high spirits at the thought of their trip to London and playing at the Royal Albert Hall. Mum beamed, proud of her girls, of their talent and the effort they put into their music.

'Will we stay with the Fords?' asked Ash. 'And will they come to the concert?'

'Yes, on both counts,' replied Dad.

'Cool,' said Ash.

'I like the Fords,' said Flame.

'Yes, they're a lovely family and good friends,' agreed Mum. 'Your father and I have known Tom and Hannah since we were all at university together.'

'I'm going to wear my new shift dress,' said Marina, dreamily. Of all the Sprite Sisters she was the one who most enjoyed clothes and fashion.

'I wonder how it will feel standing on the stage of the Royal Albert Hall,' said Ariel. 'It's a *huge* building!'

And so they went on.

Dad's announcement that he was going to look at the state of the roof after supper dampened their spirits, however.

'Is this because Oswald wants to buy Sprite Towers?' asked Ash.

'Partly – but it needs attention, anyway,' replied Dad, aware that his family was watching him anxiously. 'I don't think we can leave it any longer.'

When they had cleared the table, Dad walked out over the wide, rolling lawn, a pair of binoculars hanging around his neck, pencil and notebook in hand. Mum and Grandma followed a few minutes later. The Sprite Sisters raced around on their bicycles, as Mum, Dad and Grandma stared up at the huge expanse of the roof.

The warm evening light shone on Sprite Towers, as they walked around the house. Dad looked through the binoculars and made detailed notes. Mum and Grandma pointed out tiles that had slipped and chimneys that needed attention.

'Okay,' Dad said, finally. 'Let's go up to the attics now, and see what's happening inside.'

The Sprite Sisters put down their bicycles and followed their parents and grandmother to the top of the house.

At the top of the mahogany staircase, Dad turned left. 'Let's start at the east side.'

He marched along the corridor and opened the door of the end room. 'It's a while since I've looked at this part of the house. 'Oh Lord – look at that.'

He walked towards the wall and raised his fingers to touch a line of water trickling down the plaster.

'Yuk,' said Ariel, touching some slimy orange fungus that was growing in the corner.

'I had no idea things were so bad up here,' said Dad. 'I knew it wasn't going to look great, but I didn't expect it to be in this state. Things seem to have deteriorated.'

The Sprite family made their way around the attics. They went through the Train Room, with its huge table covered in trains and tracks, and into the Dressing Up Room, with its colourful assortment of clothes, hats and shoes.

As they progressed, Dad looked increasingly worried.

'It's worse than I had realised,' he said, staring glumly at a large, yellow patch on the ceiling. 'There's quite a bit of water coming through.'

'There were some tiles that had slipped above here – remember, we saw it from outside?' said Mum, pointing to the corner.

The Sprite family stared at another wet piece of wall.

Dad sighed heavily. 'Right, I've seen enough now. I'll get the builder round to get up on the roof and have a proper look. It's going to be a big job.'

'Let's go down, love,' said Mum, touching his arm. 'I could do with a cup of coffee.

'Can we stay a bit longer?' asked Ariel.

'OK, girls, you can stay up here for another ten minutes – bedtime in twenty minutes.'

As Mum, Dad and Grandma made their way to the kitchen, Flame looked at the line of water trickling down the wall.

'I wonder how we could use our magic powers to mend the house,' she said, thoughtfully.

'I could remove the water from the walls,' suggested Marina. 'Why don't we start with that?'

She stood in front of the wall and held up her hands, palms outstretched, over the trickle of water. As she closed her eyes, opened them and focused on her magic power, a bolt of bright blue light whooshed out of her hands. Bit by bit, she worked her way up and down the wall – and the plaster began to change colour, from yucky damp yellow to white.

'Well done,' said Flame, touching the newly-dry wall. 'But how do we stop the water coming through this bit of the roof, when we can't get up there or see the tiles from below?'

The Sprite Sisters stared at the ceiling. All they could see from inside the room were the wooden rafters and the cream-painted plaster that was packed in between.

'I think I could sense where the tiles are,' said Ariel.

'Do you think you can use your Air power to lift them?' asked Flame.

'They're heavy things,' added Marina, doubtfully.

'I'll have a go,' said Ariel.

'If you get the tiles back to the correct position, Ariel, I'll bind them,' said Ash.

Ariel lifted her hands and shut her eyes. Silently, frowning with concentration, she moved her hands in the air and used her magic power to sense the location of the tiles above her.

After a few seconds, she said, 'There's a hole here – three tiles have slipped.'

Flame, Marina and Ash watched the blue light of Ariel's magic power radiating from her fingers, as she lifted the tiles into position.

Ariel was so absorbed in the feeling of her magic, and her sisters so absorbed in watching her, that nobody heard Dad walk back up the attic stairs and along the corridor towards them. Ariel's face was tilted up towards the ceiling, her eyes were closed, her arms stretched up high above her head and her palms open flat. Her legs were braced one in front of the other and bent slightly, as if she was holding up a big weight above her head, and her bottom was sticking out, ever so slightly, when Dad entered the room.

'Ariel, what are you doing?' he said from the doorway.

The Sprite Sisters spun round in surprise.

'Oh!' said Ariel, dropping her arms instantly. Above her, there was a sudden crash on the roof, as something heavy dropped on to it.

The Sprite Sisters held their breath

'Good heavens, what's that?' exclaimed Dad, looking up.

'Pigeons,' said Ash.

'Pigeons? Don't be silly! No, it sounded like something heavy falling on the roof.' Dad stared up at the ceiling.

The Sprite Sisters waited, silent. After what felt like a very long time, Dad said, 'Oh well, we can't see it from down here.'

Then he looked round and said, 'What *were* you doing, Ariel?'

'She was giving us her impression of a praying mantis,' said Marina, quickly.

'Ri-ght,' said Dad, slowly. 'Jolly good. Very convincing – particularly the sticking-out bottom.'

Ariel giggled and her sisters smiled. It was not the first time that Dad had taken his daughters by surprise when they were using their magic powers. Had he seen the blue light radiating from Ariel's hands, they wondered. It seemed not, for Dad was looking around the room.

'What did I come up here for? Ah, yes – notebook and pencil. There they are.' He picked them up. 'Well, don't let me stop you, girls. It's very useful to know you can mimic a praying mantis at any given moment. You might be able to use it to speed up the queue in a supermarket or stop traffic.'

Dad left the room, chuckling. The Sprite Sisters burst out laughing.

'Oh fiddle!' said Ariel. 'I nearly had the last tile back in its place!'

'Quick, finish it now – I'll stand guard,' said Flame, moving to the doorway.

Ariel resumed her praying mantis stance, shut her eyes and focused her mind. The heavy clay tile hovered in the air, then dropped gently into its correct position with a gentle clunk. The hole was sealed.

Immediately, Ash stepped forward, lifted her hands and used her power to bind the repair and seal that part of the roof. As she completed this task, they heard Mum call up the stairs, 'Come down now, girls – bedtime!'

'That's good,' said Flame. 'If we keep coming up here and using our magic powers to mend the roof, we might be able to solve Dad's problem.'

And they raced down the stairs to bed.

A mile away at The Oaks, supper had been a cool, quiet affair. Glenda asked few questions and Verena had become tired of starting conversations in which her grandmother seemed to have no interest.

After supper, Glenda made coffee and carried the tray through to the sitting room. She sat down on the cream silk sofa and said, 'Verena, come and sit down beside me, dear.'

Something in the tone of her voice made Verena start – or

was it, she wondered, the fact that her grandmother had called her 'dear'? She rarely calls me that, she thought, and then only when she wants something.

Verena sat down and looked at her grandmother. Glenda smiled, but her pale blue eyes looked like ice.

She's a cold woman, thought Verena, but she's still beautiful. You can see she was once a ballet dancer: she sits so straight and bends and stretches in ways other grandmothers do not – except Marilyn Sprite. She was a ballet dancer, too, and she's very graceful.

On the coffee table in front of them was a large inlaid wooden box, ornately decorated with mother-of-pearl. Verena had never seen it before.

'Impressive, isn't it?' said Glenda, as she opened the lid and lifted out a tray.

Verena's eyes opened wide at the beautiful jewels laid out on the velvet tray.

'Yes,' she replied, staring at huge diamond rings; a pair of emerald earrings; a sapphire necklace; a gold torque with a ruby inlaid – and many, many more pieces.

'One day these will be yours,' said Glenda, quite casually.

Verena stared at her grandmother in disbelief. She was too surprised to say anything.

'Why don't you try on something?' said Glenda, picking up a strand of pearls. 'Turn around, dear, and I'll fasten this for you.'

Verena turned around, mesmerised, and lifted her hair.

Glenda placed the necklace around her neck and fastened the gold clasp.

'Go and look in the mirror,' said Glenda.

Verena stood up, walked through the hallway of The Oaks and stared in the huge gilt-framed mirror. Then she pulled back her long blond hair – and smiled at her reflection.

'To my mind, a strand of natural pearls is the most elegant jewellery of all,' said Glenda, behind her. 'See how it frames your face?'

Verena nodded, fingering the pearls. She liked the way they were different shapes and felt warm and smooth. 'They're beautiful, Grandmother,' she said.

'You will be a beauty, my dear – you already are,' said Glenda. 'And that necklace is very valuable.' Then she turned and moved back to the sofa. 'Come, Verena, let's sit down. There's something I want to tell you.'

Verena took a fleeting look at her reflection in the mirror and turned to follow. She felt elated, dreamy. She remembered how she used to put on her mother's jewellery as she was getting ready to go to a party. Her mother had always asked her to help her choose what to wear. They had laughed and played and Verena had felt happy. But now her mother was gone. She had left The Oaks and Verena, and moved to Buenos Aires to live with another man.

Verena had thought her parents were happy together and it was a blow when they parted. It all seemed to happen very suddenly. Her mother had wanted to take her to Buenos Aires, but her father had refused. They had had a big argument about it. Finally, it was agreed that Verena would stay at The Oaks and continue to attend Drysdale's, and her grandmother would look after her whilst her father was in London. Verena would fly out to Argentina in the school holidays.

She had looked up Buenos Aires on the world map. It was a long way away.

I miss Mummy so much, she thought. In two weeks' time, I shall see her again. Daddy is here so little. I wish he didn't have to work so hard in London and that he could spend more time at home.

'Did you hear a word I said?' Glenda's voice was sharp. Verena blinked, as if brought back to the real world. She knew better than to lie to her grandmother. She was like a hawk: she missed nothing.

'I was congratulating you for winning the music competition,' said Glenda.

Verena smiled. 'Thank you. I hope you'll come to hear me sing in London on Saturday.'

Glenda snapped shut the lid of the jewellery box, then turned to Verena. 'How important is it to you to win this competition?' she asked.

Verena was surprised. 'I'd love it for Drysdale's to win!'

'Absolutely,' agreed Glenda.

'Why?'

For a second there was silence. Then Verena said, in a

voice flat with disappointment, 'You're not coming to hear me sing. I knew you wouldn't.'

Glenda looked at her granddaughter. 'I haven't been feeling well since the school concert the other Saturday night.'

'I thought you were feeling better – you've been out and about this week,' said Verena. She looked down at her hands and remembered how her grandmother had been carried out of the concert hall by her uncle and Batty Blenkinsop nine days ago. She thought of the wiggly line her grandmother's shoes had made, as they scraped along the floor. The doctor had visited and told her to rest.

Verena had no idea of the truth of the matter: that Glenda's pain was the result of misusing her power. Verena knew nothing of her grandmother's magic, nor anybody else's.

'Your father will be there,' said Glenda.

'But I'm singing at the *Royal Albert Hall*!' said Verena. 'Don't *you* want to hear me?'

Glenda picked off a piece of fluff from her cashmere cardigan.

'The Sprites are all going,' continued Verena.

'That's good – they can give you a lift to your father's house,' said Glenda, crisply.

Verena stared across the room, feeling hurt and sad.

Glenda leaned back on the sofa and looked keenly at her granddaughter. 'Verena, would you like to live at Sprite Towers?'

Verena looked round at her grandmother. 'You asked me

that last Saturday, after the rounders match. I said that the Sprites lived at Sprite Towers.'

'And we talked about the fact that you are a Sprite, too.'

Verena nodded. She remembered Marina Sprite telling her this on Saturday. She did not believe her at the time. The idea that she, too, was a Sprite was surprising.

'As you know, Oswald has told the Sprites he would like to buy Sprite Towers,' said Glenda. 'The house is badly in need of repair and Colin Sprite does not have enough money to pay for it. Your uncle thinks this is a good time to press him – and I agree.'

Verena looked at her grandmother and waited.

'Oswald wants to turn the house into a hotel and build new houses in the grounds,' said Glenda.

Verena said nothing.

'I'm a director of Oswald's property company.' Glenda paused, as if thinking about this, then said, 'Oswald does not know it yet, but I intend to get Sprite Towers for us. *We* will be the Sprites living at Sprite Towers. I have enough money to buy the place and maintain it.'

Verena sighed and twisted her hair round in her hand. 'I'd rather live here at The Oaks with Mummy,' she said, staring at the carpet. I would like to live with Daddy too, she thought, but not in London, as he is never at home. Sometimes I wonder why he's always working.

Glenda stretched out her right hand and studied her long, manicured nails. 'There's something I want you to do,' she said. 'Something that may help us get hold of Sprite Towers more quickly. I have no doubt that I will own it, but I'd like it to be sooner, rather than later.'

'How can you be sure you'll own it?' asked Verena.

'Because if I want something, I always get it,' said Glenda.

This was not strictly true. Glenda had got almost everything that she wanted in her life. She'd had four husbands from whom she had gained vast sums of money. She had led a fabulous, luxurious life and been a well-known ballet dancer. She had a son, Stephen, Verena's father, of whom she was fond. Most important, she had magic power. That she loved more than anything.

There were two things Glenda had coveted, but failed to obtain in her life. The first was to be the prima ballerina in her *corps de ballet*, forty-five years ago. That honour, however, was bestowed upon her distant Sprite cousin, Marilyn. The second thing was to gain the love and property of Sheldon Sprite, another distant cousin and the owner of Sprite Towers – but he fell in love with, and married, her rival.

That she had failed to obtain these two things irked Glenda. They irked her so much that she hated Marilyn Sprite – still hated her to this day.

Marilyn Sprite stood in my way, thought Glenda. Now I will stand in hers. I will take the Sprite family's beloved home and throw them all out.

She laughed, quietly. Verena watched her, fascinated and afraid. There was something strangely hypnotic about her grandmother. It was the sense that she would stop at nothing to get what she wanted.

'The other day you asked me to spy on the Sprites,' said Verena.

'Yes – and that's what I want you to do,' said Glenda, smoothing her hair. 'I want you to make friends with the Sprite Sisters – get into the house and tell me everything you find out about them.'

'But that's not honest!' said Verena.

Glenda gave a short, cynical laugh. 'Probably not,' she agreed. 'But since when did honesty get anyone anywhere?'

Verena stared at her grandmother, horrified by her remark.

'I want you to tell me about the house, about the things the girls do when they are together,' continued Glenda. 'I want you to tell me if you see or hear anything unusual.'

'Like what?'

'Watch and listen, Verena,' said Glenda. 'There *is* something unusual about the Sprite Sisters.'

'What sort of "unusual"?'

'You will know what I mean when you see or hear it, believe me.'

'I don't know how you expect me to be friends with them,' said Verena, her voice rising. 'Flame hates me – and I hate her. She was furious when I turned up at the rounders match on Saturday. We'll never be friends and she'll never let me be friends with her sisters. It's a silly idea!'

Glenda's silence was complete and ominous.

Verena held her breath. She touched the pearls, as if for reassurance.

Finally, Glenda said, 'I don't care *how* you do it, Verena, but find a way into Sprite Towers – and make sure you can keep going back.'

'And what if I don't?'

'Then I shall move away and you'll have to leave Drysdale's and go to live in London with your father,' said Glenda. 'And I shall be very angry, Verena – very angry indeed.'

Verena stared silently into space. Then she shrugged and said, 'Okay, I'll try.'

'Good, that's the spirit,' said Glenda. 'You can keep the necklace if you want.'

'Oh,' said Verena, quietly. 'Thank you.'

A few minutes later, Verena climbed the stairs to her bedroom and got ready for bed.

I don't want to annoy Grandmother, she thought. I'll have to do what she asks, or she will go – and I don't want to leave Drysdale's . . .

She looked around the big, empty bedroom. I like Mrs Sprite and I know that she likes me, she thought. I wouldn't want to hurt her . . .

As she brushed her teeth, she thought about Marina and Ash, and how they had taken her down the garden to see their animals after the rounders match. She had been touched by the girls' friendliness.

Maybe I should make friends with Marina, she thought. I'll never make friends with Flame, and I don't want to. Marina's in the year below, but she's fun and it would annoy Flame like crazy if I became friends with her sister.

Verena smiled. It would be fun to annoy Flame, she thought, and I don't suppose I'll find out anything about the Sprites that will hurt them. Maybe Mr Sprite will find the money to mend the roof and Grandmother will give up her idea of living there.

Verena rolled over in her bed, still wearing the necklace.

Marina and Ash told me we were distant cousins, she thought, closing her eyes. I have other family nearby. Maybe I am not as alone as I feel.

And with that, she fell asleep.

Downstairs, in the gathering dark, Glenda stared out at the garden of The Oaks. In her mind, however, she saw Colin Sprite looking up at the roof of Sprite Towers, his face taut and worried.

That's it, she thought. The roof – that's the way to cripple the Sprites. They won't be able to afford to live there if the roof falls in.

She flexed her long hands and focused her mind. Then, using her dark magic, she created images of water dripping down the walls of Sprite Towers. She felt her power seep through the tiles on the roof, in between the timbers and into the very fabric of the huge, old house.

CHAPTER THREE

VERENA MAKES
A MOVE

VERENA DID not waste time. When Flame saw her approach Marina on the Quad at school on Tuesday morning, she knew, for sure, that something was up.

As Verena smiled at Marina – and, as Marina smiled back – Flame felt the hairs on the back of her neck stand up. She felt jealousy mixed with a distinct sense of unease – and of foreboding.

Marina trusts people too easily, she thought. She lets down her guard. But something's not right. What does Verena *really* want? Glenda Glass has some part in this, thought Flame. She knew it, instinctively.

She clenched her jaw and walked past the two chattering girls. Marina saw her, but carried on talking to Verena: it made her smile to think she could unsettle her older sister. It was usually Flame who unsettled her. She loved Flame dearly, but the thirteen months between them and their very different temperaments made for a level of rivalry.

Flame was passionate and intense and loved ideas and innovation. She also had the gift of foresight and could see ahead. Flame could read situations in a millisecond. She could look across a room and know who was friends with whom, and who wasn't, and who *would* be friends with whom.

Marina, on the other hand, often wished Flame would be more trusting. Flame's ability to read people irritated her at times. Marina had a natural empathy and understood how people felt and accepted things the way they were. She was also blessed with an easy warmth, that appealed to both teachers and friends and made her easy to get along with.

As she walked towards the science labs, Flame shifted her attention to Glenda. Although the Sprite Sisters had dealt with their enemy effectively at the school concert, they knew she would be back.

If Glenda *has* asked Verena to get close to us sisters, which sister would she choose, wondered Flame. Marina, of course. Although Verena and I are in the same year at school, there's been too much hostility between us for her to try to make friends with me. Ash and Ariel are too young – so Marina is the obvious choice.

I must warn her, thought Flame – at the same time sensing her sister would not accept the warning. She won't see it . . . besides, Verena is clever enough to know not to criticise us. One thing everybody at Drysdale's knows is that we Sprite Sisters are absolutely loyal to one another.

In that moment, Flame felt as if Verena had opened up a little chink between the sisters – as if she had got through their circle of protection. She felt it as a small stabbing feeling, just underneath her ribs, and she caught her breath.

There are cracks in Sprite Towers' roof – and now there's a small crack between us, she thought, placing her hand across her abdomen.

And there was something else that troubled Flame. Verena is a Sprite, she thought, and she may have magic powers like her grandmother. What do we do then? Or what if she hasn't, but she finds out that we do, and exposes us publicly? Our magic powers would vanish . . .

It was a hot afternoon. At home time, the Sprite Sisters climbed into Mum's big red car and opened all the windows. Mum turned on the engine and pushed back her wavy blond hair from her pretty face. A few seconds later and they were homeward bound, the breeze blowing through the car as they drove along.

'Verena's grandmother's not going to the concert, Mum,'

said Marina, who was sitting in the front next to her mother. 'Can we give her a lift to London on Saturday morning? She's staying with her father.'

'Yes, of course, darling,' said Mum, steering the big car round a bend. 'Tell Verena we'll be leaving at ten-thirty, sharp.'

'Thanks, Mum,' said Marina. 'I'll tell her.'

Flame's heart sank. She knew Mum would say that giving Verena a lift was the right thing to do – and that there was nothing *she* could say without looking spiteful and mean.

Sitting in the second row of seats, Flame and Ash glanced at one another. 'At least Glenda's not coming to the concert,' Ash whispered.

Flame leaned forward and said, 'Mum, how will we all fit in the car with Verena and our instruments and bags?'

'It'll be a bit of a squash and the cello case will have to go on the roof-rack,' replied Mum. 'But we'll manage – we always do!'

Mum stared at the road ahead as they headed out towards the country. She had bigger issues on her mind. The matter of Oswald Foffinton-Plinker's intentions was worrying her.

We *do* always manage, she thought. There will be a way to fix the roof. There *must* be.

She looked up in the mirror and saw Ariel's reflection. Sitting on the back row of seats, her youngest daughter was miles away, her face tilted up to the wind coming in through

32

the open window. Ariel was thinking about how she had used her magic power to lift the fallen roof tiles back into place the night before. She was just about to say something about this, when she remembered she Must Not Say Anything About Her Magic in front of Mum.

It is hard to remember, she thought, and it feels strange that I can't tell Mum about my magic power.

'Can I turn on the radio, please?' Marina asked Mum, in the front.

'Yes, love,' replied Mum.

A few seconds later, they were all laughing as they sang along to a favourite song. Marina turned in her seat and smiled at Flame. Flame smiled back, quickly, then looked away.

'We'll do music practice straight after tea today, girls,' said Mum.

As soon as they got in, the Sprite Sisters sat down to drink homemade lemonade and eat Grandma's freshly-made fruitcake. Then they got out their instruments and music stands and sat in a semicircle in the dining room. The three older girls played stringed instruments: Flame played the violin, Marina the viola and Ash the cello. Ariel played the flute. Mum stood in front and conducted them.

For the next hour, they practised their pieces for the music competition.

'Perfect!' said Mum, as they finished. 'Only four more days to go! It's so exciting!'

Mum went to help Grandma prepare supper, while the girls put away their instruments. Then Ash and Ariel dashed out to the garden to feed their animals. Flame and Marina tidied up the music stands.

'I noticed you and Verena deep in conversation several times today,' said Flame, casually. 'It must have annoyed Janey that you've suddenly got a new friend.'

'Verena's not as bad as you make out,' said Marina.

'She is Glenda Glass's granddaughter,' said Flame, turning to face Marina. 'Have you forgotten what Glenda did to us?'

'It wasn't Verena who hurt us,' replied Marina, meeting her gaze. 'She seems a bit scared of Glenda. She's funny, Flame – and we seem to get on well.'

'Funny? Verena Glass?' said Flame. 'I've never seen it. I know that she has Glenda's blood running through her veins – so she's part of the bad side of the Sprite family.'

'I think you're making a fuss about nothing,' said Marina. 'Stephen Glass is a good man – Mum and Dad like him a lot. So that side of the family can't all be bad.'

'Are you doing this to get at me in some way?' said Flame, her face colouring.

'Doing what?' asked Marina, putting her hands on her hips.

'This buddy-buddy stuff with a girl I've been at war with ever since I started school – that's what!' said Flame.

'We're not joined at the hip, you and I, Flame! I am allowed to make my own friends!' said Marina.

'Fine!' said Flame. 'But don't you realise that Verena probably has an ulterior motive for this sudden display of chumminess – and it's not necessarily your attractive personality that's making her talk with you, but her grandmother who's put her up to it?'

Marina was surprised and wounded by this remark. She stared at Flame, holding back tears, and had just opened her mouth to retaliate when Mum came into the dining room.

She saw her two elder daughters facing one another, both looking upset. 'What's going on?' she asked.

'Nothing,' Flame and Marina replied in unison.

Mum waited, but they both seemed reluctant to speak. 'Well, whatever it is, just cool it, please.' She turned and went back to the kitchen.

Flame and Marina looked at one another, warily.

'I'm sorry,' said Flame. 'I didn't mean to be unkind.'

'That's okay', said Marina.

'We need to use our magic powers to do some more roof repairs,' she said. It was typical of her to think of this, even when there were other things bothering her. Flame always remembered the things they needed to do. It was a quality her sisters found irritating – it sometimes made her bossy.

'Good idea,' agreed Marina, nevertheless, keen to change the conversation.

'Just be careful with Verena – please, sis,' said Flame, touching Marina's arm as she turned.

'Yeah, yeah,' said Marina. 'Shall we do the roof now or after supper?'

'Better wait till afterwards,' said Flame and the two sisters went into the kitchen to lay the table for supper.

The Sprite family sat down to a supper of crunchy cheese and vegetable crumble and leafy green salad, tossed in Mum's famous oil and garlic dressing.

'Yum,' said Ariel, tucking in.

'It's nice to think we grew all the vegetables that are on this table,' said Ash, thoughtfully. 'It's very satisfying to grow things. I think that's what I'll do when I grow up.'

'I hope you will, Ash – you're a wonderful gardener already.' Her father smiled at her. The two of them spent many happy hours together in the vegetable garden each week.

'What time did you tell the Fords we'd be there, Ottalie?' Dad asked Mum.

'Around two o'clock,' she replied. 'The concert starts at six-thirty. Oh, and I've agreed we'll give Verena a lift. We'll have to drop her off at Stephen's house in Chelsea, en route to Fulham.'

'Yes, Stephen rang me to say thank you,' said Dad. 'He'd like to take us all out to lunch on Sunday at a chi-chi restaurant overlooking the river.' He smiled, anticipating his daughters' reaction.

'Fantastic! Wow, Dad! We can go, can't we? Pleeease!'

Marina, Ash and Ariel all said at once. Flame was silent.

Dad looked at Mum. She was the one who organised things. 'What do you think?'

'That would be nice,' she said. 'I was thinking we could go to the British Museum on Sunday morning.'

'Good idea,' said Dad. 'Stephen and Verena may like to join us there. We can have a late lunch and come straight home.'

'I wonder what I should wear on Sunday,' mused Marina.

While the sisters chatted about their clothes, Dad said to Mum and Grandma, 'It's not often we leave Sprite Towers empty.'

'It'll be fine, Colin,' laughed Mum. 'We're only going away for one night!'

'If Oswald knows we're away, he may bring his cronies to look around the grounds,' said Dad, half joking.

Mum smiled. 'Oh Colin, really!'

'You may laugh, but I wouldn't put it past him.' Dad stabbed a lettuce leaf with his fork. 'Oswald has a lot of tricks up his sleeve.'

The Sprite Sisters heard this and all looked at Dad.

'Do you believe that, Dad?' asked Ash.

'Well, I know he wants to take a good look at the house,' said Dad. 'So far I've refused to let him come. He may take the opportunity while we're away. I suspect he wants to take a closer look at the roof – work out what we'd have to pay to get it repaired.'

Flame looked up suddenly as Dad said this. She had the sense of something – something dark, like a shadow – moving around the grounds. For the second time that day, she had a sharp feeling underneath her ribs and placed her hand on her abdomen. She said nothing, but her unease was not lost on Grandma.

'Everything all right, love?' asked Grandma, looking round at Flame – and knowing it wasn't. She and Flame often sensed things together.

'Yes, fine, thanks,' smiled Flame, knowing Grandma knew it wasn't, but that this was not the time to say anything. They smiled at one another as if to say, 'We'll talk about this later.'

'Perhaps I should stay here and look after the house,' Grandma suggested to Mum and Dad.

'No, Grandma, no!' Ariel and Marina shouted.

'You've got to come and hear us play in London!' said Ash at the same time.

'The house will be fine, Marilyn,' said Mum. 'Colin, please stop worrying about it and winding everyone up.'

Dad raised his hands. 'Okay, I give in,' he smiled.

At the other side of the big kitchen table, Marina whispered to Flame, 'Can we put some magic around the house before we go?'

Flame nodded. 'Good idea,' she whispered back.

'Who's looking after Bert?' asked Ash, referring to the family sausage dog.

'I'm sure my friend Joan will have him,' said Grandma. 'She loves Bert.'

'Pudding will be fine. We'll leave him some water and dried food – and he can go out and catch a few rats,' added Mum. Pudding was the large grey cat that spent much of his time asleep on the Windsor chair beside the Aga. Despite his lazy appearance, Pudding was a fearsome rat-catcher and much valued at Sprite Towers.

After supper was cleared, the Sprite Sisters went up to the attics. The first thing they checked was the ceiling where Ariel had moved back the roof tiles the evening before, in the east room.

'Eeeh,' shivered Ash. 'There's a really strange cold feeling in here.'

'Yes,' agreed Flame. 'It didn't feel like that so much yesterday. I wonder what's happened?'

Again, the shiver ran down from her ear through her spine – but she said nothing.

Marina climbed up on a chair and placed her hands on the plaster. 'It feels drier,' she said. 'I'll take out the rest of the moisture in this bit.' For the next minute, her magic power whooshed out of her fingers. Then she climbed down and said, 'There we go.'

'I'll apply some heat through it,' said Flame, climbing on the chair. Within another minute, the wall had dried back to its original white colour.

For the next hour, the four sisters made their way around the whole room. Ariel put the tiles back into their correct position on the roof above them; Ash bound them into position, so they would not slip again; Marina dried out the water that had come through the holes and Flame warmed the plaster back to its original colour.

When they had finished, Ariel and Ash scanned the roof for any more gaps using their magic power.

'I think we've done it – the roof here is in good repair now,' said Ash.

'That's fantastic!' said Flame. 'I knew we could do it!'

'How many rooms are there up here?' asked Ariel.

'Eight,' replied Flame.

'Seven more to go then,' said Marina. 'We should have the whole roof mended in no time at this rate.'

The Sprite Sisters were standing there, admiring their magic handiwork, when Dad walked in.

'You're not still practising praying mantises, are you?' he chuckled.

'No, we were – um – we were looking for some dressing-up clothes we thought we'd left in here,' said Flame, quickly.

'I thought I'd come and check the roof,' said Dad, moving across the room to the corner where Ariel had mended the first hole. 'This is one of the worst rooms – though there is water pouring in on the room at the west end.' He placed his hands flat on the wall – then stepped back in surprise.

'The plaster's warm!' he said. 'Yesterday it was cold, damp and yellow. Now it's cream and dry – and warm!'

He looked around at his daughters, mystified. It did not occur to him, for a second, that they had anything to do with this, as he knew nothing of their magic powers.

'Same thing here,' he murmured, holding his palm flat against the wall in the next corner. 'How very odd!'

Dad stepped back and rubbed his chin, thinking. The Sprite Sisters remained silent. Flame grabbed Ariel's arm in case she forgot she must not tell him about her magic power. Ariel jerked her arm back and gave Flame a cross look.

'Maybe I've got the wrong room,' said Dad. 'I don't think so, though. I could have sworn it was this room – I wrote it down. Let's go and look in the others.'

They all moved to the next attic room, which they found as they had seen it the night before. It was the same for all the other rooms.

'Okay, let's leave it for now,' said Dad. 'I think I'll just pop down the garden and check if I can see that bit of the roof from outside.'

'We'll come with you, Dad,' said Ash.

They hurried down the stairs and into the garden, Dad stopping briefly to pick up his binoculars. He marched across the wide lawn, his long legs making big strides. The Sprite Sisters ran beside him. Finally, Dad lifted the binoculars to his eyes and looked up at the roof of the huge house. 'Good Lord!' he muttered.

41

'What is it, Dad?' asked Marina.

Dad put down the binoculars, then gave a short laugh. 'Your mother noticed some tiles that had slipped, at the end of the east wall. Now it looks as if they've moved back up! It defies gravity! Up there – see.'

The Sprite Sisters all wanted to see their magic work and took turns to look through Dad's binoculars. They looked very pleased with themselves and grinned at one another.

Mum and Grandma walked over the lawn towards them in the evening sunshine.

'Come and see this!' Dad waved to them and handed Mum the binoculars.

She lifted them to her eyes. 'Good heavens! But *how*?' she asked.

'I have no idea,' said Dad, shaking his head.

'It's a miracle,' said Mum quietly, handing Grandma the binoculars.

Grandma held the glasses up to her face, looked carefully, then turned to smile at her granddaughters. She knew how the roof had been repaired – and they knew she knew.

'Well done,' she said to Flame, as they walked back over the lawn in the evening light. 'It's what Sidney Sprite would have wanted.'

'How do you mean?'

'Well, you're not aware of it yet, but this house and its grounds are magic,' said Grandma. 'It follows that Sidney would have wanted it maintained by magic. Do you remember what I always tell you?'

'That nothing happens by chance?' asked Flame.

'Yes.'

'So?'

'Think about it. Ariel has turned nine and you all have your magic powers, now. At the same time, Sprite Towers is under threat. You have to use your magic to save the house.'

Flame nodded. 'I'll talk to the others,' she said. They were silent for a moment, then Flame said, 'Grandma, I keep getting this feeling . . .'

'What, love?'

'I think Glenda Glass may be trying to get at us again.'

Grandma made a noise like a low growl. 'Then we must be on our guard,' she said.

'All right, bedtime, girls,' said Mum, as the Sprite family piled into the kitchen. Just then the telephone rang. Dad answered it and handed it to Marina.

'It's Verena,' he said. 'She wants to talk with you.'

'Don't be long, Marina – it's getting late,' said Mum.

Marina took the phone, aware that her three sisters were watching her. 'Hi,' she said, then walked off to talk in the drawing room.

Flame's mood dropped like a stone.

In the hallway, Ash and Ariel were about to climb the wide mahogany staircase.

'Night, Sidney!' they both said to Sidney Sprite's portrait, which hung at the bottom of the stairs. It was a long-held family tradition that the Sprites said goodnight to Sidney on their way up to bed.

Flame followed and heard Marina say, 'Bye' on the phone. Her sister came out of the drawing room and closed the door behind her.

Flame said nothing. As she walked past, she looked at Marina with an anxious face and carried on up the stairs.

'Night, Flame,' called Marina.

'Night,' said Flame.

CHAPTER FOUR

MRS DUGGERY ARRIVES

MUM HAD just finished giving a piano lesson at Sprite Towers on Thursday morning, when the doorbell rang.

She lifted up the heavy iron latch and opened the front door. Outside stood a tiny, very, very old lady with piercing eyes, a lilac knitted hat and big brown boots.

'Good morning,' said Mum, brightly.

'Mornin',' replied the old lady in a broad Norfolk accent, staring Mum hard in the eye.

Mum's mouth opened slightly, in surprise.

'I'm Mrs Duggery and I understan' you want some help,' said the tiny old lady.

'Help?'

'In the house.'

'Oh, I don't think so!' Mum smiled politely.

'I heard you needed help, so I come,' said Mrs Duggery, with absolute certainty.

'Oh!' Mum was taken aback. 'Who would have told you that?'

'As soon as I heard, I come – so I's here,' Mrs Duggery repeated. She crossed her tiny arms over her tiny chest.

'But we don't need any help,' said Mum.

'Well, I wouldna' come if you dint,' said Mrs Duggery, her eyes glinting. She stood square to the door as if she was not going to budge.

'Er – well, hold on a minute, please,' said Mum. 'I'll just see if my mother-in-law knows anything about this.'

She closed the door slightly and went through to the kitchen. Grandma was sitting at the big oak table, doing her newspaper Sudoku puzzle. Bert the sausage dog lay curled up by her feet.

'Marilyn, have you said anything to anyone in the village about needing some help in the house?' said Mum, coming into the kitchen.

'No dear, why?' replied Grandma, looking up.

'There's a strange old lady standing at the front door. Insists she's heard we need some help – and that "she's come",' said Mum. 'Says her name is Mrs Duggery.'

'Mrs Duggery?' Grandma put down her newspaper and

pencil. Then she said, 'Good Lord! *Mrs Duggery!* I haven't heard that name in years!'

'Who is she?' asked Mum, mystified.

'She was our housekeeper when we were first married,' said Grandma, standing up. 'She looked after Colin when he was a baby.' She chuckled. 'She was an old lady *then*!'

'Well, goodness knows what that makes her now,' said Mum, following her through the hallway to the front door.

Grandma opened the door wide and stepped out.

The old lady gave a beaming smile and opened her arms wide, 'Well, bless me – thas Missus Sprite!' she said.

'Well I never! Mrs Duggery!' Grandma bent down, wrapped her arms around the old lady and gave her a big hug.

Mum looked on, much amused at this reunion.

'You mus' be the new Missus Sprite,' said Mrs Duggery, turning to Mum and holding out a tiny, very wrinkled hand.

'Yes,' smiled Mum and shook it. 'Please come in, Mrs Duggery. I'll make some coffee.'

'Thank you, that I will,' said Mrs Duggery and she clumped through the front door. She stood, for a moment, in the hallway of the big old house and looked around and up the stairs.

'Ah,' she said. 'Thas nice ter be back, that is.'

Grandma watched her, smiling. Mum looked on, bemused.

'I see yer still got the master there,' said Mrs Duggery, pointing to Sidney Sprite's portrait on the wall. 'He's watchin' over the old house, to be sure.'

'I am sure he is,' agreed Grandma. 'Come on through.'

They walked through the library to the conservatory – Grandma tall and elegant, with her long, dancer's strides and Mrs Duggery clumping along in her heavy brown boots. In the conservatory, Grandma opened the doors that led out to the garden, then they sat down in the big wicker chairs.

In the kitchen, Mum filled up the kettle and put it on the Aga hob. Five minutes later, she carried a tray of coffee and chocolate biscuits through to the conservatory.

Grandma and Mrs Duggery were rattling on like old friends. Despite the warmth of the room, Mum noticed that Mrs Duggery kept on her lilac knitted hat and seemed to be wearing a large number of cardigans.

'Mrs Duggery's offered to come and help with the house-work,' said Grandma, as Mum sat down. 'We could do with a hand for a bit, don't you think, dear? There are those big old cupboards in the attics that we've been meaning to turn out for months, but haven't found the time.'

Mum held her cup of coffee and sat silent and amazed. How could Mrs Duggery possibly do housework, she wondered. She didn't look as if she was big enough to pick up a fly swatter, let alone turn out cupboards full of old furniture!

'I'll settle up with Mrs Duggery – so don't worry about that,' continued Grandma. 'And she has very kindly offered to stay at Sprite Towers while we go away this weekend, so we won't need to worry about the animals.'

It was no good, Mum realised. She would have to agree to this. Objecting to Mrs Duggery's help would offend her mother-in-law.

'Okay then – thank you,' said Mum. She smiled at Mrs Duggery, who nodded and took a large bite out of her third chocolate biscuit.

'Thas all settled then,' she said.

Mum thought the old lady seemed to smile, but it was difficult to work out what she was thinking. Her face had so many lines in it and her expression was so – so inscrutable.

'Where do you live, Mrs Duggery?' she asked.

'Round about,' replied the tiny old lady, swigging a large mouthful of coffee and taking a fourth biscuit.

'Oh,' said Mum, baffled. She looked at her mother-in-law for clarification – but Grandma just smiled at her as if this was all perfectly normal.

'How did you get here?' asked Mum.

'On me bicycle,' replied Mrs Duggery, dunking what was left of the fourth biscuit.

'Oh,' said Mum. 'And have you any family, Mrs Duggery?'

Mrs Duggery nodded and took her fifth biscuit.

'Mrs Duggery is a Sprite, Ottalie,' said Grandma.

'A Sprite?' said Mum.

'That I am. My mother, Elisa, was Sidney Sprite's younger sister,' said Mrs Duggery. Then she stood up. 'Right, thank yer for the coffee an' biscuits. Now I's brought me apron. Where would yer like me ter start?'

Mum looked at Grandma in astonishment. Grandma jumped up and smiled at Mum.

'I'll come up with you, Mrs Duggery,' she said, and the two Sprites walked out of the conservatory.

Mum sat in her wicker chair for a while, looking out at the garden and pondering how life at Sprite Towers was full of surprises.

The Sprites are a strange lot, she thought.

'We've got a new addition to Sprite Towers,' Mum said, smiling rather mysteriously as she drove the girls home from school.

'What? Who?' they all asked at once.

'A lady called Mrs Duggery,' said Mum. 'She's come to help Grandma sort out the attic cupboards. She is very old – in fact your grandmother says she looked after your father when he was a baby. And she's a Sprite.'

Ariel smiled and looked out of the window as the car pulled through the gates of Sprite Towers.

'What's she like?' asked Ash.

'You'll soon see,' said Mum, smiling. 'She is ... *unusual* – and she is very fond of chocolate biscuits.'

The four Sprite Sisters piled out of the car and in through the front door, their faces bright and eager.

Mrs Duggery seemed to know they were coming, as she was standing, waiting, in the hallway.

Flame, Marina and Ash stopped – and stared. Ariel, however, walked forward, offered her hand and smiled at Mrs Duggery. The tiny old lady took her hand and shook it.

'Sidney told me you were coming,' said Ariel.

Mrs Duggery said nothing. She simply nodded and gave Ariel an inscrutable smile.

Flame, Marina and Ash looked at each other, then at their sister.

What is Ariel talking about, wondered Mum. She says some very strange things.

The three older sisters shook hands with Mrs Duggery. They gazed at her lilac knitted hat and looked down at her large brown boots. Then the tiny old lady turned and said, 'Right, well I'm off now,' and clumped towards the open front door. 'Yer mother-in-law and I've made a start on the cupboards,' she said to Mum. 'See yer termorra then.'

'Oh, right – thank you, Mrs Duggery,' said Mum, standing aside. 'See you tomorrow.'

They all watched as the tiny old lady picked up a heavy, old boneshaker of a bicycle, which had been lying against the front wall. They stared, amazed, as she climbed on to it and cycled off, her tiny legs going like pistons, up and down on the pedals.

As Mrs Duggery set off down the middle of the long drive, Dad roared up the drive in his old sports car, saw her approaching, swerved and narrowly missed hitting her.

Mum and the four Sprite Sisters gasped in horror – but

Mrs Duggery carried on, as if nothing had happened.

Dad scrunched to a stop in front of the house, got out of his car and shouted, 'There's a mad old woman in a strange hat cycling down our drive! I nearly killed her!'

'That's our new addition to the household!' said Mum, laughing. 'Come on, let's have a cup of tea and I'll explain.'

As the Sprite family walked through the house, Flame stood at the front door watching the tiny figure of Mrs Duggery recede down the long drive.

She has come to protect Sprite Towers, she thought. Which means that something is about to happen . . .

There was no time that evening for magical roof repairs. There were now only two days to go before the finals of the National Schools Music Competition and Mum insisted on two hours of practice after supper. That done, the Sprite Sisters went up to bed. Once Mum and Grandma had said goodnight and gone downstairs, Marina, Ash and Ariel crept through to Flame's room and sat on top of her bright red duvet.

'Did you notice how many cardigans Mrs Duggery was wearing?' said Ash. 'I counted at least eight!'

'I think her lilac hat is cool,' said Ariel. 'I think I'll get one.' This was met with howls of derision from her sisters.

'Do you think she's a magic Sprite?' asked Ash.

'She might be – how amazing would that be!' said Marina.

'A good magic Sprite or a bad magic Sprite?' asked Ariel.

'If Grandma likes her, she must be a good Sprite – especially if she's going to stay while we're away,' said Ash.

'Yes, that's true,' said Marina. 'Why do you think she's here, Flame?'

'I think she's come to protect Sprite Towers,' replied Flame in her authoritative, older-sister voice.

'Why?' asked Marina.

'Do you think something will happen while we are away?' asked Ash.

'Yep,' nodded Flame. 'That's exactly what I think. And we all know who will be nearby while we are in London.'

'Glenda,' said Ash, biting her lip. 'Oh heck.'

Flame, Ash and Ariel looked at Marina.

'What?' she said. 'Why are you looking at me like that?'

Flame, Ash and Ariel were silent.

'Oh, you're not going to start going on again about Verena, are you?' said Marina, her voice rising.

'You seem to be getting very friendly with her,' said Flame. 'I keep seeing you together.'

'Well, I like her!' said Marina.

'Her grandmother doesn't like us,' said Ariel, in a small voice. 'She hurt us and she frightened me.'

Marina drew a breath. 'I know, pumpkin, but Verena is not her grandmother,' she said, taking Ariel's hand.

'Just be careful, please,' said Flame.

'I've had enough lectures, thanks. Goodnight!' Marina climbed off the bed, stomped across the room and banged the door shut behind her.

'She's angry, because she knows I'm right and that bugs her,' said Flame.

'Maybe you're worrying too much about Verena,' suggested Ash, quietly.

Flame clutched her legs in front of her and put her chin on her knees. 'No, I don't think so. I have a hunch there's something behind Verena's sudden attention.'

'Mrs Duggery will look after Sprite Towers,' said Ariel, dreamily. 'Sidney told me so.'

'Oh, you and Sidney!' teased Flame, tapping Ariel's leg.

'He *did*!' said Ariel. 'He told me Mrs Duggery would surprise us!'

'Well, she certainly gave Dad a surprise this evening!' said Ash and they all laughed.

Five minutes later, Ash walked back to her bedroom along the second-floor corridor of the huge house. She was thinking about Verena and Glenda Glass.

She got into bed and stared around the dark room, then touched her cheek. She felt the long, narrow scar that was now healing. She remembered the searing pain she had felt as the cello string snapped in the concert two weeks ago, and cut her. Glenda Glass had caused that to happen. She remembered the fear she and her sisters had felt as they sat on the stage. She thought about the dark power that Glenda had hurled at them, and how they had formed the Circle of Power to stop her.

I'll get Glenda back for that, she thought. I know Grandma says we shouldn't use our magic to hurt people, but there must be something I can do. I don't want to hurt Glenda, but I would just like her to know we haven't forgotten what she did to us. Maybe when the wound on my face has healed, I shall forget about it.

Then she rolled over and went to sleep.

Stillness settled over Sprite Towers as the evening turned to night. Downstairs in the huge, stone-floored kitchen, Mum, Dad and Grandma sat and talked about the house, Oswald's offer and the fast-approaching trip to London. With such a lot on their minds, they were a thoughtful group.

Then Dad said, 'Do you really think Drysdale's could win the music finals against such stiff competition, Ottalie?'

'Absolutely,' replied Mum, holding her mug of coffee close to her. 'I talked to Dick Taylor, the music head, yesterday, and he's confident. The orchestra is on top form – and our girls played beautifully this evening. They seem more relaxed than they were before the first concert.'

'That's good news,' said Dad. 'Well, why don't we just forget about the roof and Oswald for a few days and enjoy the weekend?'

'Good idea,' agreed Mum.

'And you can relax about Sprite Towers – Mrs Duggery has offered to look after everything,' said Grandma.

'Marvellous,' said Dad.

CHAPTER FIVE

ASH'S SECRET

ASH GOT up very early on Saturday morning and crept out of the house before anyone else was awake. She ran down to the stables to collect a bucket, then across the lawn, past the Wild Wood, towards the Big Field.

There, she climbed over the railings and jumped down on to the dewy grass. For a moment she stood and enjoyed the still, sweet air of an early summer morning, then she started to look carefully at the grass.

There they were.

Grasshoppers. Grasshoppers everywhere!

It was as if there'd been an explosion of the long-legged

insects. Ash had noticed them the day before and formulated her plan.

She put down her bucket and kneeled down on the grass, taking care not to squash any grasshoppers. Then she lifted her right hand, called in her power and cast some binding magic over the bucket. Anything she put into it now would stay there until she removed the magic.

Around her, on the grass, the green and brown insects rubbed their huge back legs together. They had bulbous black eyes and long antennae, and they made a gentle 'rurrppy' noise.

Ash moved her hands over the grasshoppers around her and cast her magic power. Now, instead of jumping away, they would stay still on the ground. Using her thumb and forefinger, she picked them up one by one and placed them carefully in the bucket. Soon she had collected a hundred grasshoppers.

Ash smiled. The whole bucket seemed to be going 'rurrppp'.

Then she leaned over the bucket, held her hand over it and said, 'Ssh, please, grasshoppers, I need your help. Someone needs to be taught a lesson.'

With that, she stood up, picked up the bucket of now silent grasshoppers and walked, as fast as she could, back to the house.

She did not want anyone to see her with the bucket. Of all the Sprite Sisters, she was the one who most liked to do things on her own. Usually, they did their magic together, but there was something about this that Ash just knew she had to do alone.

She walked beneath the Conker Tree, then to the west wall of the house. There, she hid the bucket underneath a bush.

It'll be fine here for a while, she thought, then went back down the garden to the stables. A few minutes later, as she filled up the rabbits' water bottles, Marina and Ariel ran down the garden to help, their faces bright and shining.

'I'm all ready. Are you packed?' asked Marina.

'I'm packed but I need to change,' replied Ash, stroking her little brown and white rabbit, Fudge. She looked at Marina's pretty new dress and said, 'You look nice.'

'Thanks,' said Marina, pleased. 'Dad's going to put your cello case on the car roof-rack – we will look funny, driving along!'

'Oh, it's *so* exciting going to London!' said Ariel, jumping up and down.

At eight-thirty a.m., the Sprite family gathered in the kitchen to eat a quick breakfast. Then Grandma dashed off to the hairdresser's, just as Mrs Duggery arrived on her bicycle. Dad and Ash went down to the vegetable garden to water everything that needed watering, while Mum sorted out the packing. Flame and Marina were putting overnight bags and musical instruments into Mum's big red car, when a sleek black car glided into the driveway, swooshed around the gravel in front of the house and stopped in front of the dining room window.

Flame looked up. 'Verena's here,' she called to Marina.

The doors of the car opened. Oswald Foffington-Plinker and Glenda Glass got out and stood, for a moment, looking up at the huge old house. Verena got out of the back of the car, looking stunning in the latest designer gear. She walked towards Marina, smiling.

'Hi!' she said, swinging an expensive cerise handbag and pulling a lime travel case behind her.

'Hi!' said Marina, gulping at the sight of Verena's attire.

Oswald and Glenda started to walk towards the house.

Marina looked at Glenda and drew a sharp breath. For a second, she remembered what this woman had done to her and her sisters, but Verena had hooked her arm under hers and was propelling her towards the front door.

Flame stood beside the red car, watching Glenda – and she felt anger rising inside her.

This is the woman who tried to hurt my sisters and me, she thought – and now she is walking towards our *house*.

Feeling the intensity of Flame's gaze, Glenda turned, unperturbed, and looked at the tall, copper-haired girl with the long legs.

She is just like her grandmother, she thought – the same shape, the same intensity of character, the same green eyes.

'Mum's inside,' Marina said, turning to Oswald and

Glenda, as she opened the front door. 'Come in.'

Mum was coming down the wide mahogany staircase carrying two suitcases, when Oswald and Glenda walked through the front door after Marina.

She groaned quietly to herself. Oh gawd, she thought – not now! Not them! We're all busy! But Mum was unfailingly polite.

'Good morning!' she said, brightly and turned to Verena. 'Hello there, dear!' she smiled. 'Are you all ready?'

Verena beamed back. 'Yes – thank you so much for taking me!'

It was clear that Mum was busy, but Oswald and Glenda did not move. So, Mum being Mum, said, 'Would you like a cup of coffee?'

'That would be lovely, Ottalie,' smarmed Oswald. His black hair was slicked back with gel and the ends flicked up over his neck. He wore an expensive navy blazer and a huge gold watch on his left wrist.

Glenda stood, tall and elegant, in a beige silk dress with matching ostrich-skin bag and shoes. She smiled coolly and nodded, as if the invitation was what she expected.

'Marina run and put the kettle on please – and you and Verena, please don't disappear,' said Mum, pushing her soft blond hair off her face and wishing she looked smarter. 'We have to leave at ten-thirty, sharp.'

'Okay, Mum,' said Marina.

'Where is Marilyn?' asked Glenda, looking around the huge hallway.

'At the hairdresser's – she'll be back soon,' replied Mum, then she turned and said, 'Flame, please fetch your father.'

'Where is the old boy?' asked Oswald.

'Just checking the vegetable garden – June is a busy month for produce,' said Mum.

'Well, why don't I pass on the coffee and go and find him,' said Oswald. 'I'd like to have a look at the garden while I'm here.'

Flame looked sharply at Oswald. You planned this, didn't you, she thought.

Mum glanced at her with a face that said, 'Don't leave *him* wandering about here!'

Flame understood. 'I'll take you, Mr Foffington-Plinker – don't want you to get lost. Follow me.'

'And I'll go and make the coffee,' Mum said to Glenda. 'Let's have it in the conservatory.'

Glenda smiled. 'Do you think I might use the loo?'

'Of course – it's right here,' said Mum, pointing to the cloakroom door at the side of the hallway. 'I'll be with you in a moment. The conservatory is through there.' She pointed to the library door.

'Thank you,' said Glenda.

Two minutes later, Glenda came out of the cloak-room. Mum was in the kitchen. Verena and Marina had disappeared. She was alone in the hallway.

Hmm, she thought, time to explore . . . And she walked to the bottom of the wide mahogany staircase and looked up.

It's a magnificent sight, she thought, looking up at the ornately-carved banister that ran up and up for two floors, right through the centre of the house. On the walls, she noticed the portraits of Sprite family members in heavy gilt frames.

She turned to gaze at the portrait of Sidney Sprite, which hung at the bottom of the staircase. She gave Sidney an ironic smile then, clutching the banister rail, turned to go up the stairs – but stopped.

Suddenly, as if from nowhere, a tiny old woman in big brown boots and a lilac knitted hat had appeared on the staircase right in front of her.

Glenda blinked in surprise. There was something about the old woman that seemed familiar – something from way back, but she couldn't put her finger on it.

'The conservatory's tha' way – through the library,' said Mrs Duggery, pointing down.

'Thank you,' said Glenda, staring at Mrs Duggery. 'I was just admiring the staircase.'

Mrs Duggery's eyes glinted.

Glenda's path was blocked. She looked again at Mrs Duggery, then turned – and saw that Ariel had been standing behind her.

The youngest Sprite Sister looked up at Glenda, her heart thumping: she had walked in through the front door and seen Glenda about to climb the stairs.

'Mummy's through here,' said Ariel, pointing to the kitchen.

With Mrs Duggery in front of her and Ariel behind, Glenda conceded.

'Show me the way to the conservatory, dear,' she said, following Ariel through the hallway.

'In here,' said Ariel, opening the door to the library.

Glenda sat on one of the huge wicker chairs and gazed out at the garden. The conservatory was filled with pots of brightly-coloured geraniums and orchids and a huge yucca plant, twelve feet high.

I *want* this house, she thought. I *want* Sprite Towers – and I aim to have it. I shall come back this evening and see around it properly later, when the Sprites have all gone.

'Here we are!' said Mum, carrying in the tray of coffee and biscuits. For the next fifteen minutes the two women sat and talked – about Verena, the house, the garden.

Mum sipped her coffee and looked at Glenda. She looks remarkably like Marilyn, she thought.

But where her mother-in-law was kind, Glenda gave her a shivery feeling down her back. She noticed, too, that Glenda kept the conversation away from herself – and neatly avoided answering Mum's questions about her.

Mum liked people. She was a kind and caring soul, but however hard she tried to like Glenda – and try, she did –

she felt uneasy. There is something about her that you just couldn't trust, she thought.

Meanwhile down in the vegetable garden, Oswald was eulogising about Sprite Towers. Dad listened but wanted to finish the watering.

Where did Ash go, he wondered. She disappeared when Oswald turned up.

Oswald chortled on. 'Wonderful place, old chap! Absolutely spiffing! Sprite Towers and its grounds will make the most terrific development.'

'Oswald, I've *told* you it's not for sale!'

'Don't look so *worried*!' said Oswald, jovially, bashing Dad on the arm. 'I'm going to make you a *very* rich man.'

Dad was so incensed by this remark that, for a moment, he thought about squirting Oswald with the garden hose to get rid of him – but rescue was at hand.

Ariel came running over the lawn towards them. 'Mum wants you to fix the cello to the roof-rack and she says we're leaving in fifteen minutes!' she shouted.

'Righty-ho,' said Dad.

'Where's Ash?' asked Ariel.

'She was here, but she vanished. Oswald, I must go in.'

'Another time,' said Oswald. 'Can't let you be late – Drysdale's must win the concert tonight, eh?' And he turned to smile at Ariel.

Ariel looked up at Oswald. He was a big man, almost as

tall as her father. His hair is all greased back and I don't like him, thought Ariel.

In the conservatory, Glenda and Mum finished their coffee as Grandma returned from the hairdresser's. She walked in, saw Glenda, stopped, nodded at Glenda and said to Mum, 'I'll go and get my bag down.'

Glenda Glass nodded at Marilyn Sprite, tight-lipped.

Mum was still surprised at the coolness between the two women, which she had first noticed at the school concert two weeks earlier. She sensed there was something between them that she did not understand.

'Where's Ash?' Mum asked Grandma, as she walked away.

'I expect she's out by the car. I think we're ready to go as soon as Colin fixes the cello.'

'I must just tidy myself up and put on some lipstick,' said Mum. 'It's been a very busy morning.'

Outside the front of Sprite Towers, the big red car was already piled high with eight bags, two stringed instruments and a flute. On the roof of the car was Ash's cello.

'Have we got everything?' asked Dad. 'All the instruments – bows, spare strings, music?'

'Yes, I've checked all that,' said Mum.

'Everyone got their bag?' Dad looked round at each of his daughters and Verena, who all nodded.

'Okay, hop in,' he said.

One by one, they all climbed in. It was a squash, but nobody minded. They were in high spirits – off to London to win the competition and to have a wonderful weekend.

'All aboard!' said Dad, as he turned the ignition key.

'Bye, Mrs Duggery!' shouted Ariel, waving at the tiny old lady, who stood in the open front doorway.

Mrs Duggery nodded and gave a hint of a smile.

'Off we go!' said Dad.

'Hurrah!' everyone shouted.

Oswald gave the Sprites a wave and they waved back. Glenda watched as the big red car pulled away, then walked towards Oswald's sleek black motor.

Mrs Duggery went inside and closed the front door of Sprite Towers.

Glenda stood by Oswald's car and stared at the front door. What *was* it about the tiny old lady, she wondered.

'Strange woman to have as a housekeeper,' muttered Oswald, as he fastened his seatbelt.

'Yes, very,' agreed Glenda. 'Not quite human,' she said, almost to herself.

'How d'you mean?' asked Oswald, as he switched on the engine.

'Oh, nothing,' said Glenda, looking out of the window. 'The whole family is a bit odd.'

As they sped down the drive after the Sprites' car,

Glenda pictured Mrs Duggery shutting the door of Sprite Towers. I wonder if she is staying there, she thought.

Ahead, in the Sprite car, everybody was talking – except for Ash. She turned round in her seat to watch Oswald's car purring down the drive behind them.

At the end of the driveway, Dad turned right along the road that would take them to London. Oswald and Glenda turned left into the country lane that would lead them back to The Oaks.

Ash smiled to herself. In another few minutes, things should get very interesting in Oswald's car, she thought . . .

She looked down at her hands, spread her fingers wide, then wiggled them about. She could feel the binding magic she had placed on the grasshoppers beginning to lift.

I hope Grandma won't be cross with me, she thought. I know I am only meant to use my magic for good things – but this is not a bad thing. It's a *funny* thing.

She wiggled her fingers again. There was something deliciously nice about being naughty, sometimes, she thought.

When Oswald had walked down the garden towards her father, Ash knew this was her cue. She ran over the lawn, then moved stealthily round the side of the house and picked up her bucket of grasshoppers from under the bush.

Then, very carefully, crouching as low as possible, she crept round the corner of the house to the side of Oswald's car and opened the back door.

As her sisters went in and out of Sprite Towers with their luggage, Ash tipped the motionless grasshoppers into Oswald's car and pushed them under the front seats.

There was not a second to lose. Any moment she might be spotted by Verena – or, worse, still, by Oswald and Glenda. With a quick swoosh of her fingers, she reinforced the binding that would keep the grasshoppers in place, then, very quietly, closed the car door.

Her heart pounding, Ash crouched down and peered over the bonnet of Oswald's car.

The moment Flame and Marina walked inside, she dashed back over the gravel with the empty bucket. Once safely round the side of the house, she stood up straight and paused for a moment to catch her breath.

If anybody sees me now, she thought, they'll think I'm just carrying an empty bucket.

Then she hid the bucket under the bush and walked round to the front of the house.

Now, Ash sat in the back of the car, gazing out of the window at the ripening fields of barley – but her mind was on the grasshoppers in Oswald's car.

Any minute, she thought, they'll start climbing up . . .

Oswald smiled as he drove along, the cool breeze from the air-conditioning wafting over his shiny face. He'd just seen the grounds of Sprite Towers. Now he would go home and have a nice lunch with his wife Gloria.

Glenda stared ahead. She was thinking about Mrs Duggery's arrival – and whether it would scupper her plans for Sprite Towers.

Neither of them had noticed the army of grasshoppers that had begun to advance from under their seats.

As the first grasshopper hopped on to the walnut dashboard, Glenda gave a muffled scream.

'What's that?' said Oswald, trying to swipe it off.

Then another grasshopper appeared – and another.

'How on earth did they get in?' said Oswald, swiping furiously. 'We've got the windows shut!'

Glenda cringed. She felt her flesh start to creep. She was afraid of little – except insects. She felt a prickly sensation on her left foot and leaned down to rub it, felt something lumpy – and looked down.

'*Oswald*,' she whispered, sitting completely rigid in her car seat.

'What?'

'*The car is full of grasshoppers!*'

'What do you mean?'

Oswald glanced down. Grasshoppers were crawling up his jacket. They were crawling over his legs. They were crawling all over his shirt. One had nearly made it to his face.

'*Urgh!*' he said, swatting them. '*Revolting!*'

Next to him, Glenda looked as if she had rigor mortis.

For the first time in her life, she was so frightened she could not move a muscle.

A hundred grasshoppers were now hopping all over the car. Glenda gripped Oswald's arm tightly with both hands.

'*Let go!*' he shouted. 'I can't steer!'

And as he shouted, she screamed – and screamed and screamed.

Oswald jammed his foot on the brake and clutched the steering wheel. The smart black car swerved crazily along the narrow road, then came to a halt in front of a mossy green bank.

Immediately, Oswald leapt out of the car and stepped back in his expensive leather loafers – right into a pile of horse dung, lying on the tarmac.

'*Blast!*' he bellowed. He was like a mad man, swatting grasshoppers, rubbing the dung off his shoes and shouting all at the same time.

Glenda Glass opened her door and climbed out, swatting her beige silk dress. Her smooth blond hair looked like a bird's nest, as she frantically rubbed her head.

'*Get off! Get off!*' she shouted – and stepped back into another piece of horse dung lying on the road, stabbing it with her thin stiletto heel.

'Oh my beautiful shoes! They're ruined!' she cried, seeing the skewed horse dung. She frantically tried to get it off her heel, at the same time waving her hands around her head. 'Help me, Oswald,' she whimpered.

Oswald came over to her. 'Hold still,' he said, picking a large grasshopper off the top of her head. For the next few minutes Glenda stood, trembling, as Oswald picked off the grasshoppers climbing over her and threw them on to the bank.

Once they were free of the insects on their clothes, Oswald peered into the car – and winced. There were grasshoppers everywhere.

'Do you think they're doing grasshopper poo all over my leather seats?'

Glenda gritted her teeth.

'We could drive home and get the vacuum cleaner and suck the blasted things out,' he suggested.

'I don't care *how* you do it, Oswald, but I am not getting in that car until you assure me that every grasshopper has been removed!'

'Okay, keep your hair on.'

Oswald took off his blazer, rolled up his shirtsleeves and climbed into the car. Glenda leaned on the bonnet of the car, with a face like thunder.

There was only one way those insects had kept still and out of sight, she thought – magic.

Oswald hurled grasshoppers out of the open door. They hopped off on to the bank.

'The windows were shut when we drove up to Sprite Towers – or were they?' he muttered.

Then he pulled himself up and leaned against the open car door. 'How do you think they got in? How come they didn't appear till we were moving?'

'I have no idea, Oswald,' replied Glenda, brushing a fleck off her dress. 'For heaven's sake hurry up or we'll be here all day.'

I wonder which of those girls did it, she thought. The red-haired one: she was outside. It could have been her. The dark-haired one: she was with Verena. Not likely to be her. The little blond one: she came into the conservatory. What about the other one, the brown-haired girl – the quiet one?

Glenda's eyes narrowed. I didn't see her at all, she thought – and her mother asked where she was. I'll bet it was *her*.

I'll get my own back, she thought, her jaw tightening. The Sprite Sisters will all suffer for this.

Fifteen minutes later, Oswald climbed out of the car, hot, thirsty and very fed up.

'The car is grasshopper-free,' he said. 'Now can we *please* go home?'

Gingerly, Glenda peered into the car and under the soft leather seats. She opened the glove box and felt underneath the walnut dashboard.

'They've *all* gone, Glenda – *really*,' said Oswald, wearily. And he climbed back into the sleek black car and started the engine.

* * *

As Glenda climbed back into Oswald's car, the Sprites were on the road to London.

In the back of the big red car, Ash closed her eyes and smiled at the thought of Glenda Glass covered in grasshoppers. She may be a horrible woman with dark powers, she thought, but I bet she's a real wuss when it comes to grasshoppers.

From her seat at the front, Grandma looked around at Ash.

Ash looked back and swallowed hard. Uh-oh, she thought. I wonder if I've been sussed? How is it Grandma always seems to know when we've been using our magic powers? I'll get told off and I will have to promise her I won't use my magic again. Still, it was worth it, just this once . . .

And she settled down in her seat and gazed out of the window.

CHAPTER SIX

✳

MRS DUGGERY SURPRISES

✳ ✳
✳

As the the cars sped away down the driveway of Sprite Towers, Mrs Duggery shut and bolted the heavy oak front door. With Bert trotting at her heels, she walked through the hallway, her big brown boots clumping on the tile floor. In the kitchen, she placed the kettle on the Aga hob. A few minutes later, she sat down at the big oak table and drank tea and ate chocolate biscuits.

Through the warm afternoon, Mrs Duggery busied herself with various domestic tasks. She polished the brass doorknobs in the house; then she collected up all the silver ornaments and cutlery and put them on the kitchen table.

One by one, she polished each piece until it shone brightly. Then, one by one, she put back each piece in its special place, walking from room to room.

Later in the afternoon, she walked around the house and garden and had a good look at it all. She knew Sprite Towers well, though it was some years since she had been there. A smile crept across her wizened face as she thought of the happy times she had spent here, in her younger years.

She checked the girls' animals, rounded up the chickens and got them in the chicken house so they'd be safe from foxes during the night. She fed Pudding, the cat, then Bert, in the utility room. Afterwards, she gave the little dog a good run around the garden. Then she came inside again and went round the whole house, checking that each window and door was locked, before she prepared some supper.

After her meal was eaten and cleared away, and as the sun lowered in the sky, Mrs Duggery turned out all the lights in the house and went up to the guest bedroom on the first floor. There, she switched on the television that Dad had carried into the room and sat down in the pretty pink armchair with Bert on her lap. Together, in the darkening room, they watched a quiz show to which Mrs Duggery knew the answers to all the questions – and they waited.

While Mrs Duggery was polishing the silver, the Sprites were hurtling along the motorway towards London, with Dad at the steering wheel and Grandma beside him.

Flame sat behind Dad and stared out of the window. Beside her, in the second row of seats, Ariel was talking to Mum. At the back, in the third row of seats, Marina and Verena nattered away nineteen to the dozen and Ash was sitting even more quietly than usual.

As Flame stared out at the passing fields, she half-listened to Marina and Verena's chatter and felt increasingly irritated by the two girls. Each time Verena said something to get closer to Marina, she had the sensation of a shard of ice piercing her heart. She shivered slightly.

No good will come of this friendship, she thought. There is something not right here – and it's splitting us sisters apart.

But there was nothing she could do – only listen.

Flame focused her mind on Sprite Towers and the picture of Mrs Duggery standing in the open front doorway as they drove off that afternoon. Images of the lilac-hatted old lady flashed through her mind. She seemed to see Mrs Duggery standing in the kitchen doorway, as if she was guarding it, then standing in the conservatory doorway – then again, standing at one of the bedroom windows, looking out on to the garden.

Flame scrunched up her face and chewed her bottom lip. Mrs Duggery must have magic powers, she thought. That's why Grandma encouraged Mum and Dad to let her stay.

So what's going to happen, she wondered? Is this something to do with Oswald wanting to buy the house? Is Glenda in on it, too?

'You all right, Flame?' asked Mum. 'You look deep in thought.'

Dad looked in the rear view mirror and caught Flame's eye. 'What's up?' he said.

Grandma looked round at her and also caught her eye.

Flame smiled. 'I was just thinking about the concert,' she replied.

She knew Grandma would not believe that, so she smiled at her grandmother, quickly, acknowledging her concern. Now was not the time to start voicing fears about Sprite Towers.

'Do you think Drysdale's will win this evening, Mum?' asked Ariel, looking up at her mother.

'Yes – you all stand a very good chance,' said Mum. 'But the important thing is to enjoy it.'

Ash leaned forward and whispered in Flame's right ear. 'I've got a strange feeling something's going to happen at home tonight.'

Flame half-turned towards her and nodded. 'Me too,' she whispered.

'What are you talking about, Ash?' asked Marina, leaning across Verena, who sat in the middle.

'Nothing,' said Ash, turning to look out of the window.

Flame glowered at Marina, as if to say, 'Shut up, stupid!'

In the nick of time, Marina realised this must be something to do with their magic powers – and she flopped back in her seat with a heavy sigh.

Verena was all ears. What was this, she wondered? Something is going to happen? She looked from one sister to another, but they all ignored her – even Marina.

A few minutes later, Dad stopped the car at a motorway service station. Everyone got out and stretched their legs. It had been cramped, with eight of them and their luggage and instruments. As the Sprite family went to get drinks and go to the loo, Verena stuck to Marina like a limpet – so there was no chance for Marina to ask Flame or Ash what they had been talking about.

Ten minutes later, after Dad had checked that Ash's cello was still secure on the car roof, they all piled in and set off again.

'Nearly there!' said Dad, as the City of London rose on the horizon. Everyone sat up.

'Look, there's the Gherkin!' said Grandma, pointing at the spiralling glass cone building that dominated the skyline.

Half an hour later, the Sprite family drove along the Victoria Embankment, the River Thames on their left-hand side. They stopped in Chelsea, to drop off Verena at her father's very smart house, then pressed on towards Fulham. With Verena gone, the atmosphere between the sisters changed immediately.

'What was that you and Flame were whispering about earlier?' Marina asked Ash.

'We've both got the feeling something's going to happen at home tonight,' said Ash, quietly.

'Like what?'

'I don't know – you'll have to ask Flame when we get there,' said Ash. 'She sees it more clearly than I do.'

'Well, what do *you* think is going to happen?' asked Marina with a frown. 'Do you feel something, too?'

Ash shrugged. 'Yeah – it's just a weird feeling I have of someone being around the house.'

Marina sat back, silent and thoughtful. Then she looked at Ash and said, 'Glenda?'

Ash nodded, screwing up her face.

'It figures,' said Marina. 'So what do we do?'

'Hope that Mrs Duggery has magic powers,' whispered Ash with a worried smile.

Finally, the Sprite family arrived at the house of Tom and Hannah Ford and their three children. The Sprite family piled out of the car and the Fords greeted them warmly. Soon, they were all sitting in the garden enjoying the afternoon sunshine and eating a delicious barbecue.

Then it was time to get ready for the concert. The Sprites all took a shower and put on their best clothes. The Ford and Sprite families clambered into their cars; Dad followed Tom's car all the way to the Royal Albert Hall.

After they had parked, they made their way towards the huge domed, red brick building. As they walked up the wide path, the two families stopped and looked up.

'Well, girls, you are about to play in one of the world's

most famous concert halls,' said Dad, holding Ash's cello. 'It's an impressive sight, eh?'

Mum sniffed and looked a little teary. Dad put his free arm around her.

'What's the matter, Mum?' asked Ariel, taking her hand.

'To think that you'll all be playing here – it's wonderful,' she said and looked round at her daughters. 'I'm so proud of you all.'

Half an hour later, the Sprite family and the Ford family were seated in the huge concert hall, surrounded by over three thousand other parents, teachers and musicians. The National Schools Competition drew a wide audience, not just the people connected to the three finalist schools. In the front row sat the judges – important, well-known people who would select the winners. Three schools would compete for this year's title: Blackstone's, Walden's and Drysdale's. Drysdale's musicians would be the last school to play, so, after they had safely stowed away their instruments back stage, Flame and her sisters sat with their family in the auditorium.

At six-thirty, the concert began and, for the next forty-five minutes, the Sprite Sisters sat back in their seats and enjoyed the music. The musicians from Blackstone School were the first to play.

'Blimey, they're good!' said Marina, pulling her thick hair back from her face.

'Are they better than us?' asked Ariel.

Marina shrugged. 'They're easily as good.'

In the break, the sisters asked Mum what she thought. She was the expert musician in the family and the girls respected her judgment.

'They were *very* impressive,' she said.

The Sprite Sisters slumped.

'But so will you be!' said Mum. 'You'd expect all the schools tonight to be impressive, girls. This is the *finals*!'

After a twenty-minute break, Walden School began their performance with a resounding overture.

'Crumbs,' said Marina. 'They're good, too.'

She and Ash looked at one another and then at Flame. But Flame was distracted. She looked at her watch: 7.10 p.m. Another two hours until it's dark, she thought.

In her mind, she saw Mrs Duggery checking the locks on all the doors and windows of Sprite Towers, and then turning out the lights as she walked upstairs. She saw her sitting in the guest bedroom watching television, with Bert on her lap.

The house is getting dark, thought Flame. She is waiting. What does she think will happen? Does she think Glenda Glass will harm the house while we are away? Does she know how she tried to harm us?

Her mind was full of questions, as she sat gazing at Walden School's orchestra, on the huge stage.

In the break before the next piece, Flame whispered to her sisters, who sat either side of her, and told them what she had seen in her mind.

'Are we safe from Glenda Glass here?' asked Ariel. 'I am nervous enough as it is.'

'Yes, pumpkin – I'm sure she cannot harm us here,' said Flame. 'This evening we have only to think about our music.'

'But what about Sprite Towers?' asked Marina.

'Mrs Duggery will protect the house, I'm certain of that,' said Flame.

On Flame's right-hand side, Ash whispered, 'I filled Glenda's car with grasshoppers.'

'*What!*' hissed Flame. 'When?'

'While you were packing up the car,' said Ash.

Ariel began to giggle. 'What did Ash say?' asked Marina, leaning over her.

'She says she filled Oswald and Glenda's car with grasshoppers!' whispered Flame.

Marina nearly burst out with laughter.

'How many did you put in her car?' whispered Flame.

'A bucketful,' Ash grinned.

Flame gasped.

'What did she say?' asked Marina.

'Sssh, girls,' said Mum, turning around and looking stern.

The Sprite Sisters whispered very quietly to one another, then giggled as silently as they could, which was hard. The thought of Glenda and Oswald covered in grasshoppers was hilarious. Even Flame couldn't help laughing.

As Walden School's performance reached its powerful

climax and the clapping started, the Sprite Sisters were so distracted that they almost forgot they'd be on stage with the junior orchestra within a matter of minutes.

'What are you girls laughing about?' asked Mum, as they stood up for the break.

'We'll tell you later,' said Flame. 'Come on – we must go backstage. Bye, Mum!'

'Hang on a minute,' said Mum. 'Dad and I will go with you. It's a big place and there are a lot of people here.'

'There's Verena,' said Marina, seeing her friend approach with her father.

'There's Quinn,' said Flame, spotting his dark head through the crowd. His sister, Janey, was also playing in the orchestra and her family had all come. Flame's heart jumped as she saw Quinn – then jumped again as she saw him turn to Verena and smile as he walked past. He hasn't seen me, she thought. Her heart began to sink, but there was no time to think about Quinn.

'Come on, Flame,' said Ash, grabbing her arm. 'We're on.'

Walden School cleared the stage and Drysdale's musicians came on to set up their instruments. A few minutes later, Drysdale's junior orchestra – who would open the performance – took their seats and began to tune their instruments as the audience drifted back to their seats. It was eight-thirty. Any second now, they would begin.

Sitting on the stage with the orchestra, holding her violin, Flame looked round at her sisters and smiled at each of them. Then she looked out at the magnificent auditorium.

Golly, this place is huge, she thought, staring out at the rows and rows of dark red seats. Up and up they went. There are so many faces looking at us . . .

The orchestra waited for the swish of the baton. Drysdale's young musicians were alert and ready.

Flame concentrated hard. She watched Mr Taylor, the music master and conductor of the orchestra, but had a sudden flash in her mind – the clear image of Glenda Glass walking towards the front door of Sprite Towers in the dwindling evening light.

Focus, she thought. I must focus! There is nothing I can do about Sprite Towers! Mrs Duggery will protect the house. I must think about the music!

Flame Sprite sat tall and flexed her bow arm.

We are going to win this competition, she thought, as Mr Taylor flicked his baton and they began.

Flame poured her heart and soul into playing her violin. It only seemed a few minutes before the orchestra had finished and Verena Glass was standing on stage singing in her beautiful, clear voice.

Flame and her sisters waited, holding their breath. Their quartet was next. Here they were – the Sprite Sisters, playing together at the Royal Albert Hall!

Then, suddenly, Verena had finished and they were settling into their seats. They sat in a semicircle and tuned their instruments to the note A.

'This is amazing!' said Marina, viola and bow in hand, her cheeks flushed with excitement.

'Sure is!' agreed Ash, holding her cello and bow.

'You okay?' Flame asked Ariel.

Ariel nodded, her silver flute poised and ready.

'Focus on the music and you'll be fine,' said Flame. 'Forget about all these people.'

'I wish we could make the Circle of Power, like we did in the other concert,' whispered Ariel.

'We don't have time – and we can't move the seats into a circle like last time,' said Flame. 'Just hold that same feeling in our heads. We're balanced – east, south, west and north – and we are going to play our socks off.'

The four Sprite Sisters smiled quickly at each other, as they sat on the huge stage, the lights blazing down on them.

'Okay, Sprites,' said Flame. 'One, two, three . . .' and off they went.

In their seats, Mum, Dad and Grandma watched, listened and held their breath.

Meanwhile, at Sprite Towers, twilight was falling. The air was cool and still. The fox cubs that had been gambolling about at the edge of the Wild Wood, had gone back to their earth with the vixen. On the branches of the trees, birds settled to their nightly roost. From its perch high on the lime tree at the side of the lawn, a brown owl prepared to swoop. Bats whizzed across the evening sky on their nightly forage for insects as a large silver car drove up the driveway of Sprite Towers.

In the guest bedroom on the first floor of the house, Mrs Duggery sat up in her armchair and listened. Bert lifted his head. He had keen ears and heard the soft clunk of a car door shutting and the slight crunch of a shoe on gravel.

'Sssh,' Mrs Duggery said to Bert, and touched his nose. The little dog understood he was not to bark this evening. She turned off the television with the remote, lifted Bert on to the ground, then stood up and walked towards the side of the window.

Glenda Glass walked across the gravel towards the front door of Sprite Towers. She was dressed in a black shirt and trousers and flat black shoes. Her pale blond hair was drawn back with a thick black band. She stopped and looked up, as if she was looking for a light – some sign of life in the house. The windows were bare and dark. No curtains were drawn.

Not a light to be seen, thought Mrs Duggery, peering through a gap at the side of the bedroom curtain.

Hmm, thought Glenda, it looks as if the house is empty after all. Good.

She was not expecting to find the front door unlocked, but walked towards it anyway and turned the handle. The door was immovable. She stepped back and checked the huge bay windows either side of the front door. They were locked, too.

No matter, she thought. There will be a way in, even if I have to use magic.

Upstairs, Mrs Duggery moved from room to room, as she watched Glenda Glass walk around the house, trying the doors and the windows. She stood in Mum and Dad's room at the south side of the house, and watched Glenda walk down the garden. Bert stood silently at her side.

'Right, time ter go downstairs,' said Mrs Duggery, and they moved quietly through the dark house down to the conservatory.

Glenda stood in the middle of the huge rolling lawn. She looked up at the tall, red brick house with its two towers, now silhouetted against the twilight sky. She looked round at the wonderful garden and the trees that bordered the lawn and caught the scent of roses in the air. Hands on her hips, she turned to look towards the stables and the vegetable garden.

Sidney Sprite should have asked my grandmother, Margaret, to come and live at Sprite Towers when my grandfather died, she thought. But he didn't. He said she'd gone 'bad' – that he didn't want her in the house, nor my mother, Harriet. He didn't like their 'dark' magic.

Glenda's mouth tightened and a hard, cold look passed across her face.

Right, she thought. Time to get in and have a good look around my future home . . .

* * *

On the stage of the Royal Albert Hall, Flame Sprite drew a sharp breath.

'Glenda,' she murmured.

'*What?*' said Marina, looking round. They were about to begin the next piece.

'She's walking across the lawn to the house – I can see her,' whispered Flame, quickly.

'Flame, focus on the music, *please*. There's nothing you can do from here.'

'Yes, you're right.' Flame looked at the sheet music on the stand in front of her. She breathed hard and her cheeks were flushed. Ash and Ariel looked at her, anxiously, and then at each other.

'What's the matter?' whispered Ariel.

Flame was suddenly aware of her sisters' looks. 'I'm fine.'

She lifted up her violin and rested it on her chin. In her right hand, she held her bow. Her mind seemed to be in two places at once. She was reading the music, but seeing Sprite Towers in her head.

'Please concentrate, Flame – I know it's hard, but you *must*,' said Marina.

You will *not* enter, thought Flame. You will *not* enter . . . '*Flame!*'

Flame nodded at her sister and her mind focused. Her sisters waited.

'One, two, three,' she counted them in.

And off they went into their final piece – four young,

gifted musicians playing their absolute best. The Sprite Sisters' music soared and spun and danced through the air and, at the end of the piece, they were rewarded with thunderous applause.

As the moon rose over Sprite Towers, Mrs Duggery stood as still as a statue behind the tall yucca in the conservatory. She looked tiny in comparison with the plant. She stared out between the long dark leaves, through the arched windows, and watched Glenda Glass walk towards them. At her feet, Bert growled.

'Sssh, Bert,' said Mrs Duggery. 'Be still now.'

Glenda walked on to the terrace and surveyed the elegant Edwardian conservatory, with its wooden tracery and huge panes of glass. She stepped forward to the door, took hold of the brass doorknob and tried to turn it. It would not move. The door was locked. She let go and took a step back.

Hidden in the shadow, Mrs Duggery stared at the doorknob from the inside and summoned her magic power.

Glenda held out her hand and pointed her finger at the doorknob. A bolt of dark grey light swooshed out and hit it. At the same time, Mrs Duggery sent an invisible beam of magic power from the other side.

That should do it, thought Glenda. She grasped the doorknob – but it did not move.

That's strange, she thought. I've never known my magic to fail before.

She tried again – sent another bolt of even stronger power into the doorknob.

And, as she did so, Mrs Duggery sent out her magic power – and heated the doorknob to burning point.

Glenda Glass stepped forward and took hold of the round, brass knob – cried out and clutched her hand. It felt as if it was on fire.

'What's this?' she growled. She stared into the dark conservatory, but could see nothing. '*Who's there?*'

For a few seconds, she peered into the darkness, but could see only plants.

I will not be beaten, thought Glenda.

But Mrs Duggery was one step ahead. As Glenda Glass winced from the pain in her hand, the old woman used her magic power to create a protective ring around the outside of the house. Within a moment, the walls, doors and windows of Sprite Towers were shielded from harm.

Mrs Duggery smiled to herself. This is like the old days, she thought, when Sidney and I used magic ter fight with Glenda's grandmother – when she went 'bad'. Sidney an' I saw her off – an' I'll see this one off, too.

Outside, in the gathering dark, Glenda Glass lifted her hand and pointed her finger a third time – hurling a bolt of dark power at one of the conservatory windows. But, instead of smashing it to smithereens, it bounced off like a rubber ball.

'What!' she seethed. For a moment she stared at the

window in disbelief, then she marched off round the side of the house.

With every window she tried to break, every lock she tried to force – her power just bounced off. Everything around the house had been protected by Mrs Duggery's old and very powerful magic – and nothing and no one could penetrate it.

Glenda Glass was no match for the old lady in the lilac knitted hat. She roared with fury and hurled her power, but it did no good. She could not get into Sprite Towers. And as she stood in front of the drawing room window – for she had now gone full circle around the house – she saw why.

In the light of the moon, Mrs Duggery walked forward over the drawing room carpet and stood in the bay window a few feet away from Glenda Glass. Bert was at her feet, growling.

For an instant, Glenda stood quite still.

She stared at the tiny old lady in the lilac knitted hat. Images started to take shape from somewhere way back in her own childhood. She remembered hearing the story of Violet Duggery and how she had helped to cast out Glenda's own grandmother, Margaret, from Sprite Towers.

Glenda had not seen Mrs Duggery for almost a lifetime – but she knew that the old lady had some of the most powerful magic that the Sprite family had ever known.

'*You!*' She spat out the word. 'So, you're still here, after all these years! You should have been dead a long time ago!'

Mrs Duggery watched the angry woman outside the drawing room window. Her old, lined face was inscrutable and her eyes glinted.

Glenda Glass muttered loudly and clenched her fist. The old lady stood still and silent.

Nursing her hand, Glenda turned and walked back to the car.

Then, suddenly, just as Mrs Duggery felt as if things were safe once more, Glenda Glass turned and hurled her fist in the air. A huge bolt of dark power surged out and hit the central chimney of Sprite Towers.

From high on the roof, there was a loud cracking noise followed by the sounds of crashing and banging.

Sprite Towers shook. Mrs Duggery grabbed her lilac knitted hat and felt the blow to the house as if it had been to her own body. She heard the chimney pot crash and the tiles fall.

The *roof*, she thought. I should have put more protection in ter the *roof*! Glenda's magic's already penetrated the house more un I'd reckoned it could.

In an instant, before Glenda could hurl another bolt of power, Mrs Duggery closed her eyes and used her strongest magic to protect the house from further harm. But, even as she did so, she could feel Glenda's insidious power creeping back through over the tiles and into the rafters.

As she opened her eyes, Glenda Glass stood on the

driveway and laughed. 'You see you're not invincible, old woman – and neither is this house!' she shouted and turned towards her car.

Mrs Duggery watched as the silver car disappeared down the drive, then she clumped through to the kitchen and put on the kettle.

I should have thought about the roof, she muttered to herself, crossly. Glenda's done more damage than I expected. There was more of her dark magic already in the house than I had realised – and thas workin' against me. I'll have ter see ter that there chimney in the mornin'. Now, reckon I'll have one of them chocolate biscuits with my cuppa tea . . .

'What about you, Bert? Would you like one?' she said. She leaned down to the sausage dog and stroked his long, silky ears. Bert chomped his biscuit with relish.

Mrs Duggery sat in the Windsor chair, holding her mug of tea. Pudding came to lie on her lap. After all the excitement, Bert decided it was time for a nap and curled up in his basket by the Aga. And there they would sit together, the whole night long.

At the Royal Albert Hall, the lights shone down. One hundred young musicians and their teachers were now gathered on the stage.

Everyone waited. Any moment now, the judges would announce the winners of the National Schools Music Competition.

The Sprite Sisters stood together, surrounded by their fellow musicians and singers from Drysdale's School on the left of the stage. In the middle, stood the musicians from Blackstone School. On the right-hand side were the pupils from Walden School.

The lights blazed. The audience waited. The musicians held their breath. The judges stood at the front of the stage, looking out towards the audience.

How amazing is this, thought Ariel. I'm nine years old and I'm standing on the stage of the Royal Albert Hall!

Ariel began to feel dreamy. Her grey eyes grew as big as saucers as she looked up at each of her sisters. She saw them smiling down at her. She looked out at the audience and saw row upon row of faces. She thought she could just see Mum and Dad and Grandma and the Fords sitting out there. She saw the chief judge standing at the podium. As if in a trance, she heard his deep, serious voice coming in and out of her mind. She heard him say, 'Wonderful performances' and 'Tremendous effort'. She heard lots of clapping, then the judge speaking again – followed by another burst of clapping. She saw smiling faces and people shaking hands. She looked up dreamily at the huge bank of lights high above the stage and thought how wonderful it had been to play her flute this evening, with her sisters and her school friends, in front of all these people. She heard the beautiful, floaty noise her flute made . . .

Then she heard a scream – several screams, in fact. Not

horrible screams – but big, whoopy cries of delight. She looked up at her sisters and saw they were jumping up and down and waving their arms.

'What's happened?' she said, suddenly aware of where she was.

'We *won* – that's what happened!' shouted Marina.

Ariel blinked and said, 'Fab-fantastic!'

The lights shone down. The audience clapped and clapped. The pupils and teachers of Drysdale's School stood on the stage at the Royal Albert Hall – winners of the National Schools Music Competition. The judge handed the cup to Mr Taylor, Drysdale's head of music. The delighted music master held the cup high and everybody cheered.

'We did it!' said Ash as she hugged Flame.

Marina gave her little sister a kiss. 'Well done, pumpkin!' she said to Ariel, then turned to put her arm around Flame's shoulder. The two oldest sisters smiled at one another.

In her seat in the audience, Mum had another little weep. 'I'm so proud!' she said.

Dad and Grandma smiled at one another, clapping as hard as they could.

Meanwhile, as the moon shone brightly over Sprite Towers, Mrs Duggery sat beside the Aga and smiled. She thought of Ariel's pretty little face and her big dreamy eyes. She thought of Flame, Marina and Ash whooping with glee as the result was announced. She had seen it all in her mind.

Well done, girls, she thought. Jolly well done.

The Sprite family drove back to the Fords' house that night, proud and happy.

'Well done, girls!' said Mum, for the fiftieth time.

Finally able to relax, the Sprite Sisters suddenly felt tired. Ariel curled up against Grandma. Ash curled up against Mum.

Flame stared out at the streets of London, as Dad wove his way through the traffic. Despite her elation at their success, she felt uneasy. She still had the nagging feeling that something had happened that evening at Sprite Towers. It would be too late to ring Mrs Duggery – and anyway, how could she do that without alerting Mum and Dad?

I'll just have to wait until we get back tomorrow, she thought.

With Verena gone, Flame and Marina settled into an uneasy truce – but something had changed between the sisters.

We're not balanced any more, thought Flame. We are pushing against each other, while we should be pulling together – like we did when we played this evening.

Flame looked around at Marina and caught her eye.

Marina was feeling happy, but as she caught Flame's eye, she saw in her sister's expression what she thought was anger – and she looked away. She knew what her older sister was thinking.

I like Verena, thought Marina, and I don't care what Flame thinks.

Flame turned to look out of the window, with a deep sigh.

'Nearly there,' said Dad, turning into the Fords' road. The whole family started chattering.

Inside the house, the two families drank mugs of thick hot chocolate and talked and laughed, like old friends do, until they were too tired to talk and laugh any more. Then they all went to bed and sank into deep sleep.

CHAPTER SEVEN

✴

THE SPRITES IN LONDON

✴ ✴ ✴

THE SPRITES and the Fords got up early on Sunday morning. With twelve people in the house, no one was likely to get a lie in, so Tom and Dad cooked a mountain of eggs, bacon, sausages and mushrooms, amidst much laughter and a certain amount of chaos.

Flame sliced bread and made a huge pile of toast, and was very particular that it was kept warm. Marina and the two Ford boys set the table, got the chairs, sorted the plates and put out the tomato sauce, mustard and jars of marmalade. Ash assembled glasses, cups and mugs, poured lots of orange juice and made a huge pot of coffee. Ariel and little Lily

Ford climbed under the table and played with the cats, although several times Flame told them to come and help.

Aware they would only be in the way in the kitchen, Mum, Grandma and Hannah Ford beat a retreat to the garden and sat in the sunshine drinking coffee.

And after their breakfast feast was over, they all set off for their day out.

The British Museum was bursting with visitors on the hot June morning. The Sprites and the Fords stood in the huge space of the Great Court, with its floor and walls of pale honey-coloured limestone and its spectacular sweeping roof.

'It's beautiful,' said Flame, staring up at the symmetrical glass and steel triangles that seemed to float over them. Behind the glass, the sky was blue and bright.

'I agree,' said Dad, gazing up. 'And, you know, it's the biggest covered courtyard in Europe.'

For a moment, they were lost in the elegant design of the building.

Mum, Grandma and Hannah were also looking up at the roof. Dad and Tom, who were both architects, stood and discussed the technical aspects of the structure. Marina was spinning round, watching out for Verena and her father.

'There they are!' shouted Marina, waving.

Flame's heart sank, as her sister ran towards Verena and she saw the excitement with which the two friends greeted each other.

Am I jealous, she wondered? Or is it that I just don't trust Verena?

Stephen Glass smiled cordially as he greeted everyone. Flame could see her parents and the Fords liked him. He was a tall, broad man – a 'manly' man, as her mother would say – with kind eyes. Verena looked a different girl with her father – happy and smiling.

Maybe the Glass family is not all bad, thought Flame.

The three families moved through the museum to the high-ceilinged Egyptian galleries.

'Golly, it's *huge*, Dad!' said Ash to her father, as they stared up at the colossal granite statue of Rameses the Great, an Ancient Egyptian king.

'It was built to stand outside a temple,' said Dad.

'He has a noble face,' said Ash, squeezing her father's hand.

Bit by bit, the group began to splinter off among the crowds of people milling around the galleries. 'Don't get lost!' warned Mum.

A few minutes later, Flame stood with Hannah and Lily Ford, looking at a carved stone falcon with huge talons and a fierce face. Dad and Grandma were discussing a red and cream stone carving of a strange creature that looked like a crocodile, but which was, in fact, a lion goddess. Tom Ford and Stephen Glass were wandering about chatting. Mum and Ash giggled at the figure of a cross-faced, carved stone baboon. Marina and Verena were talking too much to look at anything: Marina was admiring Verena's new Prada handbag.

As the others admired the objects, Ariel wandered towards a black granite sarcophagus. Time seemed to suddenly slow down to her, as she went into one of her daydreams. A small boy came up and stood beside her, and also stared at the huge sarcophagus, but Ariel didn't really notice him. She was looking at the stone coffin, wondering if she had enough magic power to be able to lift it – if only a centimetre – off its plinth.

It looks as if it weighs tons, she thought. I wonder . . .

Her fingers began to feel hot and tingly. She stared at the black sarcophagus and lifted her right finger in the folds of her dress, just a little, and as she did so, felt the power of Air come through her hand.

But where normal objects lifted easily with her magic, when Ariel pointed her finger, the sarcophagus lay like a dead weight.

She shut her eyes and concentrated. She visualised it rising up – and when she opened her eyes, sure enough, the black granite sarcophagus was hovering not one, but ten centimetres off its base. The small boy stared at it in complete disbelief.

'Oh my goodness!' said Ariel, astonished to see her fingers pointing at the hovering sarcophagus, and the small boy with wide eyes. Immediately, her power was broken and the black granite sarcophagus crashed down with an almighty *bang*! The whole gallery seemed to shake. Hundreds of visitors gasped and looked round in astonishment.

Ariel blinked – and knew it was time to find Mum. She merged into the crowd, as everyone stood stock-still in amazement.

'What was *that*?' people asked each other.

The small boy pointed at the black granite sarcophagus. 'It lifted up!' he squeaked.

'Don't be so silly, Henry!' said his mother, grabbing his arm and quickly leading him away, as the museum guards rushed in.

'It *did*, Mum – I saw it!' Henry protested.

'Please evacuate the gallery!' shouted the guards, herding everyone to the door.

Flame and Ash looked at one another. 'Ariel!' they both said together.

'Ariel!' thought Marina, as she looked for her sisters through the crowd.

'I hope it's not another one of Ariel's tricks . . .' thought Grandma, as she spied her pretty little granddaughter walking towards her mother.

The Sprite, Ford and Glass families came together, as the crowd moved towards the exit.

'Blimey, what a racket!' said young Ollie Ford.

'Whatever was it?' asked Stephen Glass.

'An angry Egyptian god, maybe!' chortled Dad.

Ariel stood among them, looking sweet and innocent.

Flame, Marina and Ash came up beside their little sister and were about to cart her off for a good telling off, when Mum took her daughter's hand. Ariel smiled at her sisters. She was safe for a while.

'She is the *limit*!' said Flame, her face flushing with frustration.

'What shall we do with her?' asked Marina.

'She'll expose us all and we'll lose our magic powers!' said Ash.

Verena came up beside them. 'What are you all talking about?' she asked. Somewhere in the back of her mind, she remembered her grandmother telling her there was something 'unusual' about the Sprite Sisters. 'You will know what I mean when you see or hear it,' Glenda had said. So what was happening now? Did the Sprite Sisters know who made the loud bang? A little boy had said the sarcophagus had lifted into the air – she had heard him tell his mother.

What was going on, wondered Verena. Why were the Sprite Sisters suddenly being as tight as clams? All except Ariel . . . Verena turned and caught the little girl's eye.

Ariel felt a shiver of ice pass through her, as she saw the glint in Verena's eye.

Then, suddenly, they were all outside, standing on the steps of the British Museum in the sunlight.

'Well, that was a somewhat shorter visit than we'd expected – but an entertaining one,' said Dad.

'Let's make it a longer lunch, then,' said Stephen.

'Okay, back to the car, Sprites,' agreed Dad. Tom gathered up his family. Verena went with the Sprites and her father went with the Fords.

Twenty minutes later, the three families took the lift to a restaurant high above the River Thames. When the doors opened, the Sprite Sisters gasped.

'It's really smart!' giggled Ash, as a waiter led them out to the terrace.

'Al fresco, eh,' smiled Dad. 'Jolly nice.'

'What a wonderful view of London!' said Mum.

The Sprite Sisters, the Ford children and Verena ran to the edge of the terrace.

'Look, there's St Paul's Cathedral!' shouted Ash, pointing at the big white dome across the river.

'Who designed it?' asked Dad, over their shoulders.

'Christopher Wren, after the Great Fire of London in 1666!' said Flame.

'Look, there's a police speedboat!' said Ollie Ford.

'And the Telecom Tower!' shouted Marina.

Then the six grown-ups and eight children sat down at a long table covered in a white cloth. The silver cutlery sparkled and the glasses gleamed.

Marina and Verena sat next to one another, opposite Flame and Ash.

'Let's celebrate the wonderful win our girls had at the concert, eh!' said Stephen Glass and ordered champagne.

'Would you all like cocktails?' he asked the Sprite Sisters, the Ford children and Verena. 'Non-alcoholic, of course,' he said, as Mum raised an eyebrow.

'Fab!' said Ariel.

'Yeth, pleathe!' lisped little Lily Ford.

The children studied the cocktail cards, as the grown-ups talked and laughed. The sommelier opened the bottles of champagne and filled the grown-ups' glasses.

The cocktail waiter stood, pen and pad poised, waiting to take the cocktail order. Ollie Ford ordered a Green Alien; Hugo Ford ordered an Elephant Charger. Ash and Lily each ordered a Peachy Freeze. After much giggling, Verena and Marina ordered the Alotta Colada – which was what Flame was going to order, as she liked coconut, but she changed her mind. She was not going to drink the same thing as them.

'Rose de Mai, please.' She smoothed back her copper-coloured hair and smiled at the waiter – he had lovely long eyelashes.

'Very well,' he smiled back.

Ariel stared at the cocktail menu, chewing her lip. 'And Mademoiselle?'

'Oh . . . there are so many to choose from.'

'Come on, Ariel – hurry up!' said Dad.

''ow about zee Acapulco Gold?' suggested the waiter, in a French accent. 'It eez pineapple juice, grapefruit juice, coconut cream, fresh cream et crushed ice.'

'Will it have a paper umbrella?'

'Of *course*!'

'Okay, I'll have that, please. And I'd like a purple umbrella – and lots of cherries.'

'Very well, *Mademoiselle*!'

Ariel sat back in her chair, beaming with delight.

'Right, let's order some food,' said Stephen.

Amidst all the chatter, the adults chose quickly – as did Verena, used as she was to fine dining. Hannah Ford helped her children decide. The Sprite Sisters deliberated: they enjoyed the sense of possibility; this experience was a treat.

Last to order was Ariel, as she was busy thinking of her cocktail. She noticed the cocktail waiter walking towards them across the terrace, holding high his tray of colourful drinks. She saw that each cocktail had a paper umbrella leaning nonchalantly on the side of the glass. For the second time that day, time seemed to slow down to her, as if she were in a dream. The waiter moved as if in slow motion. At the same time, her fingers tingled.

Wouldn't it be pretty if all the umbrellas twizzled, she thought – and she held up her hand as if to receive her splendid cocktail, with its crushed ice and cherries and purple umbrella.

At the same time, she felt the power of Air whoosh through her fingers and catch all the umbrellas on the tray.

As if blown by an invisible wind, the eight umbrellas spun round in their glasses. The waiter gasped, stopped, held his tray in mid-air – and croaked, '*Mon Dieu!*'

At the other end of the table, Grandma looked round and saw the umbrellas spinning – and Ariel's hand, poised in mid-air. Oh no! she thought. Instantly, she rose from her seat, as much to distract everyone as to get to Ariel as fast as she could.

The family turned as Marilyn Sprite pushed back her chair and suddenly stood up. Then they looked the other way and noticed the cocktail waiter, immobilised and staring at his tray.

'*Alors, vite, Arnaud!*' barked the head waiter, as he walked past.

Arnaud looked up, saw the faces of the diners and gasped. He drew a sharp breath, made the instant decision that the spinning umbrellas were a trick of the light and that he must get his eyes tested – and proceeded to the table.

'*Voilà, Mademoiselle!*' he said, handing Verena her Alotta Colada.

Ariel was about to receive her Acapulco Gold when Grandma grabbed her hand and said, 'Ariel, come with me, please – we must go to the Ladies before we eat.'

Ariel stood up, aware of the sharpness in her grandmother's voice, and followed her.

Flame, Marina and Ash looked at one another in horror. What's happened now, they wondered – and then realised that Grandma must have seen Ariel use her magic power. Nothing else would have made her so angry. Their faces turned to thunder at the thought that their little sister could be so stupid as to play tricks in public – again.

Verena watched, fascinated at the change in the Sprite Sisters. Something is going on here, she thought.

The adults carried on talking. Thankfully, nobody but Grandma had seen the twizzling umbrellas.

'I need to go to the loo – are you coming?' Verena smiled to Marina.

Marina caught Flame's eye – which registered alarm. Verena must not overhear Grandma talking to Ariel, on any account.

Marina was quick thinking. 'Oh, let's go in a minute – we've only just got these yummy drinks! Besides Grandma and Ariel are in there at the moment.'

She smiled at Verena, who sat back in her chair, even more convinced that, whatever was 'unusual' about the Sprite Sisters, their grandmother knew about it.

In the ladies' loo, Ariel sobbed. She had never seen her grandmother so angry.

'Do you *want* to endanger your sisters?' she asked.

Ariel shook her head.

'Do you *want* to lose your magic power?'

Ariel shook her head again.

'What have I always told you about using your magic, Ariel?'

'That we must not use it in public and not for fun,'

Ariel said quietly.

'Well, what were you thinking of out there – that *silly* trick with the spinning umbrellas!'

Grandma looked upset.

'I don't know – I just go all dreamy and my fingers tingle. I didn't mean to hurt anyone.'

At that moment a lady came into the toilets. She smiled at Grandma and looked down at Ariel, as she brushed away a tear on her face.

'Now wash your hands and let's go and have lunch,' said Grandma. She looked in the mirror and smoothed her pale strawberry-blond hair, as Ariel washed and dried her hands. 'Ready?'

Ariel nodded.

'Come on, then,' smiled Grandma. 'And remember what I told you.'

At the table, Flame had the increasing feeling that Verena was watching them very, very closely.

What really worries me, she thought, is that Marina does not seem to realise just how closely we are being observed. And what's worse is that even if I had the chance to warn her she wouldn't listen . . . She's not listening to me. She only hears Verena . . .

She smiled a worried smile at Grandma as she and Ariel sat down at the table. Grandma looked back with a face that said, 'It's all okay.'

'Everything all right?' asked Mum.

Ariel nodded, grabbed her cocktail and began to drink through a curly red straw.

Grandma smiled at Mum, then raised her glass of champagne.

'Here's to the girls and their wonderful achievement last night, winning the competition,' she said in a commanding voice.

'Hear, hear!' said the others, turning towards her. 'Well done, all of you!'

The tension was defused. Ariel sat like an angel for the rest of the lunch, enjoying the food and the sunlight and the company.

Flame enjoyed it too, but she did not let her guard drop for an instant, under the watchful gaze of Verena Glass. Once or twice she overheard the name 'Quinn', as Verena talked softly to Marina – and her hackles rose. At these times, she got up to look over the balcony to the amazing view of London and soon her spirits were restored.

When lunch was over they all thanked Stephen Glass for wonderful meal. He said goodbye to his daughter. The Sprites said goodbye to him and to the Ford family. Then the Sprites and Verena Glass climbed back into the big red car and they made their way back to the country.

CHAPTER EIGHT

THE WEEPING WALL

It was early evening when the Sprites dropped off Verena at The Oaks.

Glenda Glass stood in the front doorway of the big house and smiled at the Sprite family as if nothing were amiss. Grandma noticed Flame's hands clench in her lap as Glenda waved them off, Verena standing beside her.

Images of the tall woman with cold eyes passed through Flame's mind, as they drove away. She 'saw' her standing outside Sprite Towers in the moonlight.

I forgot all about it, she thought. I should not have forgotten . . .

Flame looked round and caught Grandma's eye. A smile passed between them. Whatever Flame was worried about, she knew her grandmother had sensed it and would talk about it as soon as possible.

Then they were hurtling up the leafy driveway towards Sprite Towers.

'Nice to be back,' said Mum, as she climbed out of the car.

Mrs Duggery opened the front door and stood waiting, in exactly the same position as they had left her the day before.

'Hello, Mrs Duggery,' smiled Mum. 'Thank you so much for staying. Is everything okay?'

'Yes, thas all fine.' Mrs Duggery smiled her flinty smile.

'Jolly good,' said Mum.

Ten minutes later, when all the bags and instruments were in the house, Dad and Ash walked down to the vegetable garden to do some watering. Ariel and Marina ran down to the stables to check on the rabbits and guinea pigs. Mum and Flame took the bags upstairs. Grandma and Mrs Duggery walked outside to the Rose Garden and sat down on a wooden seat.

There the old lady in the lilac knitted hat told Grandma about Glenda Glass's night visit to Sprite Towers.

'She's after the house,' said Mrs Duggery. 'She wants Sprite Towers.'

'What shall we do?' said Grandma, alarmed.

'Be careful, thas what,' replied Mrs Duggery. 'She has

powerful magic – and it's dark, dark. And she'll hurt the girls if she can.'

'This is frightening,' said Grandma. 'It seems Glenda will stop at nothing. We just saw her, when we dropped off her granddaughter. She looks so normal. No one would ever guess – but you and I know better.'

'Yes, my dear, that we do,' said Mrs Duggery. She had always had a soft spot for Marilyn Sprite and knew all about her fight with Glenda Glass, many years ago.

'It's a test for the girls,' said Grandma.

'That it is,' agreed Mrs Duggery. 'If they want ter live at Sprite Towers, they mus' be able ter protect it. There's a lot of magic here ter take care of, though they don't know it yet.'

'They are still very young,' said Grandma.

'They will have ter learn quickly,' said Mrs Duggery.

The two women sat silently on the bench, surrounded by white rambling roses.

Then Mrs Duggery looked at Grandma. 'There's something else you need ter know.'

'What's that?'

'Glenda had a go at the roof, as she left. Took me by surprise and knocked off one of the chimney pots – smashed a hole through the roof.'

'This is dreadful!' said Grandma. 'Whatever shall we tell Colin and Ottalie?'

'Well, I managed ter fix the inside timbers and plaster and get the pot back on the chimney, but I wasn't able ter mend the external parts,' said Mrs Duggery. 'There's somethin' funny goin' on up there.'

'I know Colin is very worried about the state of the roof,' said Grandma. 'It's old now and needs attention and we haven't the money to repair it.'

'Thas not just how old it is, Marilyn,' said Mrs Duggery. 'Glenda Glass has put some powerful dark magic inter it. And there's somethin' else going on as well. Sidney Sprite built magic inter Sprite Towers and it protects the house – and us. But this quarrel between Flame and Marina – it's throwin' the magic outer balance, thas a problem too.'

Grandma looked around at the roses. The lines on her face seemed to etch deeper and her clear green eyes seemed to cloud. She sighed heavily.

Mrs Duggery watched her, her dark eyes glinting.

'You're saying that Sprite Towers is less protected than it was?'

'Yes,' nodded Mrs Duggery. 'I dunno how Glenda Glass knows it – but she knows more about the house than I'd reckoned. She'd already put her power in that there roof and she's manipulatin' the house's magic to work against itself. That's why it can't be completely mended.'

Grandma looked at Mrs Duggery. 'That's terrible news! I told you about Oswald Foffington-Plinker's offer to buy Sprite Towers, didn't I?'

'Yes, my dear.'

'He wants to turn it into a hotel,' said Grandma, sadly.

'I'm sure Glenda is behind it, though.'

'Reckon you're right there,' agreed Mrs Duggery.

They were silent again.

Then Mrs Duggery said, 'The girls' magic needs ter be in the fabric of the house. I've done what I can today, but there's more work ter do. If the girls' power is strong enough, Glenda's dark power'll not hurt Sprite Towers. If not, then who knows?'

Grandma looked at Mrs Duggery. 'I'll talk with them as soon as I can.' Then she looked up at the sky and gave out a long sigh.

'I'll bet that were a lovely concert,' said Mrs Duggery.

'Yes, it was,' smiled Grandma. 'It was wonderful.'

For the next few minutes, she told Mrs Duggery about Ariel's escapades. The old lady in the lilac knitted hat smiled her inscrutable smile.

'You'll have ter watch that un,' she said.

'I know,' Grandma agreed. 'She's a little monkey at times.'

Then the two women stood up and walked towards the house.

'Thank you for your help, Violet,' said Grandma.

'Thas a pleasure.'

As the two women turned, they saw Flame coming towards them.

'What's happened?' she asked.

'Mrs Duggery had a visitor last night,' said Grandma.

'I thought so. I was thinking about Glenda all through

the concert. I didn't get the chance to speak to you on our own, Grandma, then forgot about it in all the excitement.'

Flame looked at Mrs Duggery with a sense of awe. Never had she seen anyone so tiny and so old, yet with so much energy and alertness.

Mrs Duggery looked hard into Flame's eyes. 'It happened exactly as you saw it,' she said.

'Oh!'

'Trust yer insight, young lady. Never doubt it.'

'Yes,' Flame nodded.

'You mus' work on protectin' the house, you four. You mus' stay close and work *together*. Find yer balance and then you'll find yer power.'

Flame stared at Mrs Duggery. 'I know.' She hesitated. 'Thank you. I'm having some problems explaining that to one of my sisters.'

Mrs Duggery nodded, as if she had seen it all and knew it all.

'Right, well I'll be off then,' she said. 'Good evenin'.'

As Mrs Duggery cycled off down the driveway, Dad and Ash walked back over the lawn. Dad stopped and looked up, shielding his eyes from the setting sun.

'That's funny,' he murmured. 'It looks as if there's a new hole in the roof.'

'Where?' said Ash, peering up.

'There – just beside the chimney breast on the east side,' said Dad, pointing his finger.

'Oh, yes,' said Ash. 'I don't remember seeing that before.'

'Neither do I,' said Dad. 'Flipping roof. Heaven knows how we will repair it all. The whole thing needs attention. Well, I'd better go up and take a look inside.'

'I'll come with you,' said Ash, taking his hand and beckoning to Flame across the lawn.

Marina and Ariel ran up behind them.

'Dad has spotted a new hole,' said Ash.

And the five of them went into the house and walked up and up the wide mahogany staircase until they reached the attics.

There was a strange atmosphere in the room where the chimney pot had crashed through the roof the night before. Everything looked in order, but each of them, even Dad, sensed something was not quite right.

'Um,' said Dad, rubbing his chin in the way he did when he was worried about something. 'It looks fine from in here, but the outside bit of this part of the roof *is* damaged.'

They all stood there for a moment, then Dad said, 'Let's go and look at the next room.'

On the other side of the chimney breast was the Train Room. The Sprite family's train set had been kept here since Sidney Sprite built the house. Everyone loved this room. In the centre stood an enormous table, over which were laid dozens of tiny interweaving train tracks. Model buildings – stations, farms, houses, churches – and tiny people, trees and animals were scattered over the table. Today, though, the room had a cold, unhappy feel to it. A trickle of water ran down the wall beside the window.

'Whatever is happening?' said Dad, mystified, touching the wall. '*Where* is this water coming from? It hasn't rained for weeks.'

As Dad bent down, they heard Mum calling.

'Colin!' she shouted up the stairs. 'Phone!'

Dad stood up. 'Coming!' he called back and walked out of the room.

'Quick!' said Flame. 'Let's make it right with our magic powers.'

'Stop telling us what to do!' said Marina. '*We* can see what needs to be done, too, you know!'

There was such sharpness in her voice that Flame, Ash and Ariel stopped and stared at her in astonishment.

'Keep your hair on,' said Ash. 'Flame's right. What's eating you?'

'She doesn't care about the house any more – that's what's happened,' said Flame.

'That's not true!' Marina bristled.

Ariel and Ash looked silently at Marina.

'Well, would you *please* use your power to dry out this wall before Dad comes back,' continued Flame, her face reddening and her voice rising.

Marina walked forward, held up her hands in front of the wall, shut her eyes and focused her mind on her power.

A whoosh of blue light burst on to the wall. Instantly, the line of trickling water vanished. Then she stepped back, her face sullen.

Flame walked forward, held up her hand in front of the wall and sent out the power of Fire. Within a few seconds, the wall was warm and dry.

The four Sprite Sisters stood, silent and uneasy.

'There's something I need to tell you,' said Flame.

'What?' asked Ash and Ariel. Marina was silent.

'Glenda Glass tried to get into Sprite Towers last night.'

'What! How?'

'Using her magic power, that's how,' said Flame, turning to Marina. 'Your new best friend's grandmother tried to break the windows and door locks, but Mrs Duggery stopped her. Unfortunately, she wasn't quick enough to stop Glenda smashing a hole in the roof. Apparently, she toppled a chimney. It fell into the room we've just been in.'

'I thought I felt something odd in there,' said Ash.

'Mrs Duggery got the pot back up and mended the inside, but there's still a hole on the outside – the one Dad saw,' said Flame.

'Look!' said Ariel, pointing at the wall Marina and Flame had just mended. 'There's water coming down it again.'

The youngest Sprite Sister put her palms flat on the wet wall. A large tear rolled down her cheek. 'The house is sad,' she said quietly. 'It wants us to know. That's why the wall is weeping.'

Flame, Marina and Ash stared at her in dismay.

'Weeping?' said Marina.

'Yes,' nodded Ariel.

For a few seconds, they considered this thought, then Flame said, 'Mrs Duggery told Grandma that Glenda has put her dark magic into the house. At the moment, our power isn't strong enough to protect it. Mrs Duggery said we had to work together or we could lose the house.'

Ariel and Ash started, their faces upset. 'No!' they both said.

Marina stared at the floor, then looked up and said, 'When we made the Circle of Power at the first concert, you said our power, together, was equal to Glenda's.'

'It was – *then*,' said Flame.

'So, what's happened?' said Marina.

Flame sighed heavily. 'Mrs Duggery says it's because we're not working together. We have lost our balance.'

Ash and Ariel gazed at Marina, silent.

'*What?*' she said, looking back at them. 'I s'pose you all think it's *my* fault!'

Before they could answer, Dad walked back into the room. 'Right, now where were we?'

He stopped, seeing his four daughters standing tense and silent. 'What's up? Are you fighting?'

Marina pushed past him. 'I've got stuff to do, Dad.' And she stalked out of the room.

Dad raised his eyebrows. For a moment or two, no one

moved or spoke. Then Dad bent down again beside the wet wall. For a few seconds, he held his hand in the thin column of water running down the plaster, then he stood up and said, 'I have to admit I don't know where this water is coming from. I hope the builder I've asked to come in will have the answer.'

He smiled at Flame, Ash and Ariel – and they smiled back at him. 'Come on now,' he said. 'Let's all go down. Your mother wants you in bed soon. You've got school tomorrow, remember.'

Flame and Ash walked to the door with sad faces. Ariel brushed away another tear.

As he turned out the light, Dad looked once more around the room.

'It's very, very strange,' he said quietly.

Later, when the Sprite Sisters had gone to bed, Ash tiptoed along the second-floor corridor to Flame's room. There she sat on her older sister's bed, as they talked about the weeping wall. Normally Marina and Ariel would have come through, too – but not tonight. Ariel had fallen asleep and Marina was lying in her bed, angry and hurt.

Too much had been said and the two older sisters were in danger of getting into a real fight. So Marina lay in her bed, propped up on one elbow, staring into the dark. She punched the wall with a tight fist, a ball of conflicting feelings.

On the one hand, she thought, I really like Verena – and

Verena seems to really like me. We laugh a lot together and Verena is very funny at times. Flame doesn't seem to see this side of her, though. It's as if she blanks it out.

On the other hand, she thought, Verena is always asking questions. It's as if she is constantly probing. Despite the fun we've had, I don't feel I can trust her. It's not like being friends with Janey McIver . . . I can tell Janey anything – apart from about my magic, that is. Nobody knows about that . . .

Marina gazed into the dark. Sometimes I feel sorry for Verena, she thought. We've got our family around us, but Verena seems to be almost alone. There are times when I feel protective towards her . . . Perhaps Flame *is* right, though. Maybe Verena is being manipulated by her grandmother and she's just using me . . .

Verena has good qualities and could make a good friend, she thought. I like to look on the best side of someone's nature, to give people a chance. Flame does not do that. She's not giving Verena a chance – but she is right about Glenda. And we do not want to lose Sprite Towers . . .

Marina punched the wall again, then lay back on her bed. I dare not trust Verena, she thought. She may be a good person deep-down, but I have to be careful.

In the bedroom next door, Ash sat on Flame's bright red duvet and listened to her older sister.

'Sprite Towers is under threat,' Flame said softly. 'We must get Marina to understand how dangerous this friendship is.'

'She thinks you're just jealous of Verena,' said Ash. 'I mean, you and Verena have been enemies for years.'

'She's right – I am a bit jealous,' admitted Flame, 'but I'm far more concerned that we sisters should stick together.'

'Maybe Verena doesn't know what she is doing,' said Ash. 'How d'you mean?'

'We don't know what her grandmother says to her,' said Ash. 'We do know that Glenda is manipulative . . .'

'What – Verena could be an unwitting spy?' asked Flame.

'Hmm,' agreed Ash. 'Or she may understand what Glenda wants, but has to play the game. *We* know how frightening Glenda can be, but imagine what she's like at home. Somehow, I don't think Verena is all bad.'

'I don't know, yet, if she's good or bad, but I do think she's dangerous to us,' said Flame. 'We know where we stand, but we don't know where she stands.'

As Ash crept back to her bedroom at Sprite Towers, Verena poured a glass of water in the kitchen at The Oaks. She was turning to switch off the light and go up to bed, when her grandmother appeared in the doorway.

'You haven't told me yet how your weekend with the Sprites went, dear,' said Glenda.

'Yes, I have!' said Verena, flustered. 'I told you about the concert and the restaurant.'

'What about the trip to the museum?' asked Glenda.

'Did anything interesting happen?'

Verena looked at her grandmother. She felt the older woman's eyes piercing right through her body. She did not want to talk about the Sprites, despite her fascination with this curious family.

'Can we talk about it tomorrow, please? I've got school at half eight tomorrow morning and I'm really tired.'

'Yes, of course we can,' said Glenda with a tight smile. 'But just before you go up, I would like to know what happened at the British Museum this morning. You were there, weren't you?'

'Yes,' said Verena, wearily.

'I'm curious, as there was a bit on the news about the Egyptian Galleries being evacuated, owing to a sudden loud noise. I just wondered if you'd heard anything?'

Glenda saw instantly that her granddaughter knew exactly what she was talking about. The girl's sudden start gave her away.

'Well?'

'Yes, we were there when the noise happened,' said Verena. 'It was all a bit strange. Everyone thought it was a bomb, but there was this small boy who said this huge black sarcophagus had lifted in the air, then dropped.

'Oh?' said Glenda.

'His mother didn't believe him.' Verena smiled, remembering the incident.

'And what do *you* think?' asked Glenda.

'Me? Oh, I don't know! I mean nobody could have lifted this thing up. It must weigh a ton.'

'Were any of the Sprite Sisters standing near it?'

Verena thought for a moment. 'Yes . . . now that you mention it, I saw Ariel walk away from it very quickly, immediately after the bang. Why?'

'I told you there is something very unusual about the Sprite Sisters, Verena.'

'What?'

'You will learn in time, my dear. But for now, go to bed.'

As Verena climbed the stairs to her bedroom, Glenda Glass stood in the kitchen and pondered. Her granddaughter had given her the information she sought. It was clear that the one of the Sprite Sisters had used her magic powers in public – but they had done this before, when they created the Circle of Power.

They didn't get caught that time, either, thought Glenda. Sooner or later, though, they'll get found out. And when *that* happens, they'll lose their magic powers. And when that happens then Sprite Towers will be mine for the taking, Mrs Duggery or no Mrs Duggery.

She smiled a cold, cold smile. Patience, she thought. It served me before and it will serve me again.

A few minutes later, Verena brushed her teeth realising that her grandmother had said almost nothing about the concert, nothing at all. Drysdale's had had a fantastic win of which she was a part – and her grandmother had shown little interest, other than a brief 'well done'.

I'm so glad Daddy was there, she thought, remembering how he had hugged her tight and said how proud he was of her. She felt safe near him.

Verena leaned both hands on the sink and stared into the mirror – and was struck by the look of sadness in her eyes.

What am I going to do, she wondered. I don't know if what I tell my grandmother is going to hurt the Sprites. I don't want to hurt them, but she makes me feel I don't have a choice. The Sprites are good people, Mrs Sprite and Marina especially.

Verena climbed into bed and thought back on the day. What is it my grandmother wants to know, she wondered? What is it that is unusual about the Sprites?

She thought about the incident at the British Museum and how she had seen Ariel move to her mother; then the look of anger on her older sisters' faces and they way they all stuck together, suddenly.

That was odd, she thought. It was as if the were hiding something.

Then something else happened at the restaurant. Whatever it was, it involved Ariel again – her grandmother took her off very quickly and seemed to be covering for her.

She's the one I should watch, Verena thought, sleepily. I'm curious to know, but if I find anything out, I don't know how I will keep it from my grandmother . . .

CHAPTER NINE

✳

DAMAGE AND FALL-OUTS

✳ ✳
✳

DRYSDALE'S SCHOOL burst into applause when Batty Blenkinsop announced its win of the National Schools Music Competition, at assembly on Monday morning. Cries of 'Well done!' 'Fantastic!' and 'Brilliant!' went up and the last week of the summer term got off to a roaring start.

As the staff and pupils walked out of the hall to lessons, Verena came up to Marina.

'Did you see the news last night?' Verena asked.

'No, why?' said Marina, sensing a combination of coolness and curiosity in her voice.

'There was a bit about the British Museum and the loud

bang we heard. Apparently they thought it was a bomb at the start.'

'Oh?'

Verena looked at Marina, noted her startled reaction. Then she went on, 'Yes, then there was speculation that the black sarcophagus – you know, the one we passed – had moved.'

'How can that have happened?' said Marina. She tried to sound calm, but her voice shook slightly. I'll bet Ariel moved it, she thought. We never did find out.

'Search me,' said Verena, watching her closely. 'I thought you might know.'

'Me? Why?'

'I dunno,' Verena shrugged. 'I thought you might have seen something.'

'No,' said Marina, honestly.

Verena knew Marina well enough to know this was the only answer she would get. 'Okay, catch you later,' she said and turned towards her classroom.

Immediately, Marina searched for her sisters.

'Hell's bells,' said Flame, when Marina told her. Then, 'Please be careful what you tell Verena.'

'Oh, for goodness' sake, what d'you think I am?'

'Manipulated.'

Marina gasped, as Flame added, 'Just as your friend is being manipulated – by her grandmother.'

'You cow!' spat Marina. And she walked off.

* * *

At supper that evening, Flame and Marina sat on opposite sides of the big oak table.

The tension between them was obvious. Mum and Dad's tack at such times was to defuse things. Grandma watched the girls closely. She knew exactly what this was about.

Mum was intrigued by the news from the British Museum. Experts had been flown in from all over the world to solve the mystery, she told them. The Sprite Sisters stayed quiet as she talked, though Flame, Marina and Ash looked hard at Ariel. The youngest Sprite Sister squirmed in her chair.

'They're even saying the granite sarcophagus has moved a couple of millimetres. How on earth could it move?' said Mum, prodding a piece of home-grown tomato with her fork. 'I mean, it probably weighs a couple of tons. It's very strange. Did you see anything, girls?'

All four Sprite Sisters shook their heads nonchalently. 'No, Mum,' they said.

'It's been on the radio all day,' said Mum. 'Everyone has a theory. Some people say it was a minor earthquake in London, though no seismic activity was registered in the area. Others think it was a bomb, though no device has been found or threats received. Then someone suggested levitation had been used to lift the sarcophagus.'

'Oh?' gulped the Sprite Sisters.

'I go for the levitation theory,' said Dad.

'Yes?' said Mum. 'And who would levitate a sarcophagus in the British Museum, Colin?'

'Aliens,' said Dad, stabbing a piece of cucumber.

'Aliens?'

'Hmm. Aliens with special powers, disguised as human beings,' said Dad. 'They are everywhere.'

'Right,' said Mum. 'And have you seen one of these – *aliens*?'

'Yes,' replied Dad, munching.

'Where?'

'They're here – sitting with us at the table.' He waved his fork at his daughters.

Grandma suppressed a smile and concentrated on her salad.

The Sprite Sisters burst out laughing. 'Aliens!' they shouted. 'We are aliens!'

'All children are aliens,' said Dad. 'I mean, do *you* understand them, Ottalie?'

'Nope,' said Mum. 'I can't say I do. Sometimes, I think our daughters come from another planet.'

'We like being that way, Mum,' said Marina, her blue eyes shining. 'We think it makes us more interesting.'

'And we like to keep you and Dad on your toes,' said Flame, with a large grin.

'You certainly do that!' said Mum.

For a moment, the tension between Flame and Marina defused. The two sisters smiled at one another over the table, aware that if their parents knew about their magical powers, they might well regard their daughters as alien beings.

'By the way, Ottalie,' continued Dad. 'I saw Mrs Duggery carrying a chest of drawers this morning. How on earth can a woman so tiny and old lift a large piece of furniture?'

'We've been clearing out some of the cupboards, Colin,' cut in Grandma in a matter-of-fact voice.

'Yes, but how can that woman *lift* a chest of drawers? That's what I want to know.'

'Mrs Duggery is an alien,' said Ariel.

Flame, Marina and Ash spun round. Oh heck, they thought. Now what is Ariel going to say?

'She has powers,' continued Ariel, ignoring her sisters.

'I think you're right, Ariel,' said Dad. 'Mrs Duggery definitely has alien-like characteristics. Don't you agree, Ottalie?'

'Hmm, she is a bit strange,' agreed Mum, pushing back her wavy blond hair.

'What do *you* think, Ma?' asked Dad. 'You've know Mrs Duggery all your life.'

The Sprite Sisters looked at Grandma. What would she say, they wondered?

There was silence for a moment, as Grandma considered how to respond to this question.

Then she said, 'I think Mrs Duggery is a fine, but very unusual, human being and I admit that her physical strength seems super-human, for a woman of her age.'

Dad grinned. 'Well, that's a very sensible answer, but what age is that?'

'Old. Very old,' Grandma replied, smiling.

'Ancient?' suggested Dad.

Grandma laughed. 'No, she's not ancient – but she is a great age.'

'Well, I think she's scary,' said Dad. 'She makes me jump. Keeps popping up round corners with those glinting eyes. And what's under that hat of hers – that's what I'd like to know?'

The Sprite family burst out laughing.

'A bird's nest,' said Ariel.

'A supply of iron pills for super-strength,' said Mum.

'Another lilac knitted hat,' said Marina.

'An alien brain,' suggested Ash.

Flame looked thoughtful.

'And what do you think is under Mrs Duggery's hat, Flame?' asked Dad.

'Wisdom,' said Flame.

'Wisdom? Um, that's interesting. Do you think that's why she keeps it on all the time? The wisdom may fall out if she takes it off?'

They all laughed, except Flame.

She pushed out her jaw and looked Dad in the eye.

'Well, I defer to your intelligence, Flame,' chortled Dad. 'Wisdom it shall be. Though I do think Mrs Duggery may have a secret winch under there as well, to help her with all that lifting.'

The cordiality that Flame and Marina had felt over supper

soon abated. After their meal, the Sprite Sisters went up to the attics to do some more roof repairs – but it was no good. They just did not seem able to find enough magical power to stop the trickles of water that had sprung up in several different rooms for more than a few minutes at a time.

'Our magic power is weakening,' said Flame. 'We're out of balance and it's allowing Glenda's power to get stronger.'

Still Marina seemed deaf to these words. Ignoring Flame, she carried on trying to mend the wall in front of her.

'Can't you see what is happening to us?' said Flame, her voice rising.

'Marina, please!' said Ash. 'We don't want to lose Sprite Towers.'

Marina turned to Flame, angrily. 'If you'd stop making such a fuss about Verena Glass, you and I would not be so out of balance. Then our magic would work!'

'Can't you see I'm only concerned about Verena because her grandmother is our enemy?' said Flame, her voice trembling. 'It's not *Verena*. It's *Glenda* using her that worries me. It's dangerous for us.'

Ariel started to cry.

Ash stared at the wall. 'The water is coming in again,' she said quietly.

Marina turned back to the wall and gazed at the water now running down it once more. Her magic power had lasted for only a few moments.

'The magic isn't working,' said Ash.

'Well, I don't believe it's just because I am friends with Verena Glass!' said Marina – and she stalked out of the room.

Flame, Ash and Ariel stood in the attic room, their heads hung down.

Things got worse on Tuesday morning. As they were leaving the house, Flame learned that Marina had invited Verena to tea at Sprite Towers that afternoon after school – and she was furious.

'I can't believe you have asked her here, after everything that has happened!' shouted Flame. 'You idiot!'

'I asked her last week!' shouted Marina. 'And I'm not an idiot!'

Mum came out and they all got into the big red car. Flame and Marina continued their argument, as Mum drove along the lane.

'Girls, girls!' she shouted, over the top of them. She pulled the car over on to the side of the road and stopped.

'*Whatever* is going on?' said Mum. 'If you don't stop shouting right now, you can get out and walk the four miles to school! Is that clear?'

Marina and Flame, nodded, silent and sullen.

'Now, Flame, what's your objection to Marina inviting Verena to tea?' said Mum.

Flame was silent.

How can I answer that, she thought. How can I explain

that we have magic powers and that Verena's grandmother has dark powers and is out to destroy us – and that she is using Verena as a spy? How can I tell Mum that?

'Well?' asked Mum, sharply.

'It doesn't matter, Mum,' said Flame. 'I'm sorry.'

Flame sank. Marina watched her, understanding her dilemma, but not wanting to lose this particular battle. Ash and Ariel looked upset. When Flame shot Marina a look that said, 'You *see* – you *see* what you are doing?', for a split second Marina regretted everything. She saw the sense of betrayal in Flame's eyes. In that instant, she realised that this new friendship was destroying her relationship with her sister – all her sisters – but still she did not want to admit it.

I get so fed up with Flame always being right, she thought. I know I am not right, but I am not going to say so.

So Verena came to tea. Being Verena, and having been briefed by her grandmother to find out everything she could, she suggested that she and Marina explore the house after tea.

'I'd *love* to see inside the towers,' she said, while they were alone in the garden. This was true: Verena *did* want to see the towers. It was her grandmother's inevitable questions, afterwards, that she did not look forward to.

Marina's instinctive reaction was that this was a bad idea.

Seeing her friend hesitate, Verena immediately pleaded. 'Please! It would be such fun! I have always wondered what's up there. There must be an amazing view.'

Marina could feel Flame's anger and hear her grand-mother's words of reproach if they knew she was even considering this action. The towers were a special place. Dad had made them out of bounds to the girls now that the roof was in need of repair.

Marina hesitated.

'Oh, come on, Marina!' said Verena. 'I'm going away for the summer and I'd love to tell my mother that I've been in the towers of Sprite Towers! Please!' she insisted, touching Marina's arm.

Marina sighed. 'Okay. But we'd better not get caught.'

'Why?'

'Because we are not allowed up in the towers,' said Marina.

'Why?'

'I don't know – it's just one of the rules at Sprite Towers. Dad thinks they're not safe.'

Marina and Verena stood at the bottom of the wide mahogany staircase, beside the portrait of Sidney Sprite. The house was quiet. Mum and Grandma were in the kitchen. Dad was at the office. Flame, Ash and Ariel were racing their bicycles through the woods.

The two girls were alone, and began to climb the staircase.

'What an amazing house this is!' said Verena, entranced, trailing her hand up the banister rail.

Up and up they went, until they reached the attics on the third floor. Still, they heard no one.

At the top of the staircase, Marina hesitated.

Why am I doing this, she wondered. In her heart, she did not want to go to the towers with Verena, but she felt pulled forward. It was as if some force was compelling her.

'Come on!' said Verena, grabbing her arm. 'We're nearly there! This is so exciting!'

They turned right towards the west tower and began to walk along the attic corridor. Still the house was silent.

At the end of the corridor was a small wooden door.

'Go on!' said Verena. 'Open the door!'

Marina turned the handle, her face tense with anticipation. The door opened towards them. In front of them was a spiral of narrow, rickety wooden steps.

'I'll go first, if you want,' said Verena and pushed past.

The girls began to climb. There were thirteen steps to the door of the west tower.

Verena was standing on the twelfth step and was just about to reach up and grab the door handle, when the tower door burst open.

'*Eeek!*' she screamed in surprise, clutching the wooden rail on the wall.

Behind her, Marina wobbled on her narrow step. 'Argh!' she screamed, too.

Standing above them, in the narrow doorway to the tower, was Mrs Duggery.

Verena stood stock-still, her eyes wide, her mouth open. She gawped at the old lady in the lilac knitted hat and big brown boots, as if she had seen a ghost.

Mrs Duggery's eyes glinted like diamonds. Her arms were folded tightly across her chest. Despite her diminutive size, she looked terrifying.

'What'a you doin' up here?' her voice rasped.

The two girls were unable to speak.

'Well?' she demanded.

Verena was silent. Marina said, very quietly, 'We wanted to see the tower, Mrs Duggery.'

'You int allowed up here,' said the old lady. 'You know that! Now get down, the two a you, before there's trouble.'

And with that, the two girls turned and climbed down the spiral staircase.

Marina marched angrily to her bedroom. Verena followed.

'I should not have taken you up there!' Marina said, as she slammed the door.

'Why?' said Verena. 'I don't understand!'

'I told you we shouldn't have tried!'

'I still don't understand,' said Verena.

'It's the way it is.'

For the next hour, the girls sat in Marina's room. Gradually, they settled down. In the end they managed to laugh about their encounter with Mrs Duggery.

'She looks completely bonkers,' said Verena.

'I know what you mean,' Marina giggled.

'It was as if she appeared from nowhere,' said Verena. 'Did you know she was here?'

'No. I thought she'd gone home.'

When Grandma heard from Mrs Duggery about the girls' attempt to get into the west tower, she resolved to have a serious word with Marina. Aware that Flame would be absolutely furious if she found out any other way, she first had a word with her eldest granddaughter.

'I will talk with Marina, so please do not say anything,' said Grandma. 'You may both get so heated that something comes out about Glenda and your magic powers in front of your parents. Please stay calm.'

Flame nodded.

'When I've had a word with Marina, I will talk with you all,' said Grandma.

'Do Mum and Dad know about the trip to the tower?'

'No, I haven't mentioned it, nor has Mrs Duggery – and I'm sure Marina will not say anything.'

'She'll be worried I'll have real go at her,' said Flame.

'Yes, I expect she will be,' agreed Grandma.

Meanwhile, Mum drove Verena home. Much as she liked the girl, she had no inclination to entertain Glenda or Oswald if they turned up to collect her. It was easiest, Mum decided, if she and Marina dropped her back.

As soon as they were home again, Mum went upstairs. Grandma quietly asked Marina to come for a walk.

Marina looked worried as they set off down the garden.

'Can I come, too?' shouted Ariel, racing up on her bicycle.

'No, darling, Marina and I want to have chat on our own this time,' said Grandma.

'What about?' said Ariel.

'Ariel, I will talk to you later,' said Grandma, firmly. The small blond girl understood this was not the time for questions and cycled off over the lawn.

'Let's go and sit in the Summer House,' said Grandma. They made their way across the grass to the Secret Garden. This was hidden from view from the house by a tall, neatly clipped yew hedge.

Grandma and Marina entered through a narrow gap in the hedge. In front of them were the Frog Pond and a lovely, old-fashioned Summer House. Grandma opened up the doors. The afternoon sun poured into the wooden room. They sat down on a big wicker sofa.

'I expect you can guess what I'm about to ask,' said Grandma, looking into Marina's eyes.

'Yes,' replied Marina.

'Was it wise to take Verena to the tower?' asked Grandma.

Marina shook her head and looked at her hands.

'You know, Sidney Sprite always said that there was a lot of magic in this house,' said Grandma.

Marina looked up, enquiringly.

'Mrs Duggery reminded me the other day. She said there was magic here "to be taken care of".'

'Ariel says she talks to Sidney Sprite – and that he says

there's magic in the house,' said Marina.

'Well, she's right.'

For a moment, they were silent.

Then Grandma said gently, 'Marina, what's the most important thing for us Sprites, as a family?'

'That we love and look after each other and Sprite Towers, I think,' said Marina, unsure that she'd got the 'right' answer.

'Yes, I'd agree with that.'

Marina looked at her grandmother's clear, sharp face and into her pale green eyes.

'You've given Flame a bit of a hard time, recently – but you need to think about how she really cares about us all. And how much she wants to keep us here at Sprite Towers.'

Marina was silent.

'This friendship with Verena *is* dangerous to us all,' said Grandma. 'Not because Verena is unkind, but because she lives with a grandmother who is very definitely unkind. We don't know what Verena tells her. Glenda is a cruel and manipulative woman and she is using Verena to get at us. There's something Glenda wants to find out so she can hurt us – we don't know exactly what, or what she intends to do, but I am sure that Verena is part of her plan.' Grandma frowned. 'Now it's difficult and I see your dilemma. You can't blame Verena, but nor can you completely trust her. If she found out about your magical power, who knows what might happen? So you see, Marina, Flame has good reason to feel threatened.'

Tears started to roll down Marina's cheeks. Grandma handed her a handkerchief.

'There's another thing,' said Grandma. Marina looked up.

'Mrs Duggery thinks that the magic that normally protects Sprite Towers is turning in on itself. That's why all these strange holes are appearing in the roof.'

'Why is that happening?' asked Marina, her eyes wide.

'I think it's something to do with you girls being out of balance.'

Marina stared at her hands.

'I believe it's important that you sisters pull together now,' continued Grandma. 'Oswald is after the house and he'll keep up the pressure on Dad. If the roof falls apart, then we may *have* to sell up.'

'Oh no!' cried Marina.

'Verena is going away for the summer, so use this time to get closer to your sister. Flame is really missing your friendship right now.'

Marina nodded, folding her handkerchief into smaller and smaller squares.

'A lot of responsibility comes with having magical powers, love,' said Grandma. 'You must think about what really matters – and *who* really matters. You need to learn to discern.'

'What does "discern" mean?'

'It means being able to see things clearly and make the right judgement in a situation,' said Grandma. 'It's a very important quality in life.'

'Are you saying I haven't been discerning about Verena?'

'You are only eleven years old, love,' said Grandma, putting her arm around Marina's shoulders. 'Nobody expects you to get everything right. Life is a process of learning. You never stop learning, even at my age. You are a very kind, caring girl. It's natural that you would want to be friends with Verena. In normal circumstances your friendship with her would be fine. But we Sprites are not normal, and if you want to keep your magic powers, you'll find you have to make choices in your life that most people do not have to make. That's why it's vital to know what and who really matters to you. You're lucky that you have a loving family and a wonderful home. But you and I know that you have responsibility in your life that will challenge you. So it's not all a bed of roses, despite what people may think when they see you running around the garden of Sprite Towers.'

Marina huddled up to her grandmother.

'I'm so sorry,' she sobbed. 'I didn't mean to hurt anyone.'

'I know you didn't, love.' Grandma stroked Marina's curly dark hair.

'I think Verena is quite lonely underneath.'

'Yes, I think you're right. It's such a shame her mother has gone. It must be awful having to live with a grandmother like that. But you never know – Glenda may disappear and then we can live in peace and quiet, and you and Verena can be friends. Dream of that, if it's what you want. You have to start with a dream and make it real. Dream your dream awake.'

'Yes, I will,' said Marina, rubbing her eyes with the back of her hand. 'Dream your dream awake. I like that.'

'Come on, let's go in. Your mother will be wondering where on earth we've got to. It'll be suppertime in a minute.'

They stood up. Grandma drew Marina to her and hugged her tight. 'You're a lovely, kind girl, Marina. Don't ever change.'

'Thank you, Grandma,' said Marina and a tear rolled down her cheek.

That evening, Grandma offered to get the girls settled in bed. She waited with towels as Ariel and Ash showered. Then the four Sprite Sisters sat on Marina's bed in their dressing gowns, leaning against the wall. Grandma sat down on the end of the bed.

She told Flame, Ash and Ariel what she and Marina had talked about in the Summer House. She told them what Mrs Duggery had said about guarding the magic in the house. And she told them that, unless they started to work together, Sprite Towers was at risk.

Then she asked Marina and Flame to make up. The two sisters gave each other a big hug and said they were sorry. Everybody cried and there were lots of hugs.

And then, finally, Grandma reminded Ariel once again not to play with her magic.

As the sun set over the woods and fields, the four Sprite

Sisters said good night to each other and went to their beds. Flame went to her tidy red room with its navy blue carpet and neat shelves of books. Marina snuggled down under her blue and white striped duvet, in her untidy yellow room. Ash checked the seedlings on her windowsill before she drew the curtains and settled down in her calm, green room. Little Ariel wafted away on a dreamy cloud under her pink duvet.

And Grandma walked down the wide mahogany staircase with her long, dancer's stride, carrying a laundry basket full of socks and school dresses. On her face was a peaceful and satisfied smile.

At the same time, at The Oaks, Glenda Glass blocked the doorway to her granddaughter for the second time that week.

Verena Glass stood in the kitchen, holding her glass of water, waiting to go to bed.

'You are not going upstairs until I have every last detail of what happened and what the tower looked like,' growled her grandmother.

Verena leaned back, tired, on the kitchen table. 'I told you, Grandma – I didn't see anything.'

'Well, let's just go through it one more time.' Glenda pulled out a chair.

Sometimes I wish I'd never met the Sprite Sisters, thought Verena to herself, as she sat down wearily to face her grandmother's questions.

CHAPTER TEN

※

OSWALD'S
IRRESISTIBLE OFFER

※ ※
※

OSWALD FOFFINGTON-PLINKER'S formal offer to buy
Sprite Towers dropped on to the doormat at twelve-thirty
on Wednesday afternoon. Dad was working in his office,
when he heard the letterbox snap shut. He walked through
to the hallway and picked up the mail, including a letter
addressed to *Mr & Mrs Colin Sprite*. He recognised the
expensive white envelope, made a loud 'Humph' sound
and walked back to his desk.

There, he kerflumped into his chair. He was already feeling
gloomy that morning. An early telephone call had alerted
him to the fact that his architectural practice had not won a

prized commission. The work would have secured his business and the school fees for the next two years, and gone some way to repairing the roof – but it was not to be.

And, now, here was the letter from Oswald Foffington-Plinker, which he had been expecting, but dreading. Dad stared at it for a while, then reached for the paperknife, slit open the envelope and pulled out the letter.

'What?' he exclaimed. He had expected Oswald to come up with a good offer for Sprite Towers, but the amount written on the letter was a vast amount of money.

Oswald knows we'd have to be offered a ridiculous sum to move out of Sprite Towers, roof or no roof, he thought.

Dad stared out of the window at the line of trees that ran down the east side of the garden. Through the open window he heard birds singing and the breeze rustling through the leaves. Other than that, all was quiet. I love the peace of Sprite Towers, he thought. We are so lucky to live here.

Then he looked again at the letter and the endless row of noughts on the figure.

It's an obscene amount of money, he thought, rubbing his chin.

Then he looked again.

I suppose I would need quite a bit of that, if I were to have to buy us all another house, he thought.

Then Dad began to dream.

Think of the travelling we could do, he thought. Think of the places we could see. It would be wonderful for the girls to go to different countries. We'd be secure for the rest of our lives. It's quite a thought . . .

Just then the front door opened. Mum was back from giving some piano lessons at Drysdale's.

'Hello,' she called.

'Hi, love,' said Dad, walking through to the hall, holding the letter.

'Ah,' said Mum, spotting it. 'Is that what I think it is?'

'Yes,' said Dad.

They walked through to the kitchen and sat down at the table.

Five minutes later, Grandma came home from her game of bridge, which she played every week with three old friends.

'Oh dear,' she said, as she walked into the kitchen. 'I can guess what that is. Am I right?'

'Yes,' said Mum and Dad together. Mum handed her the letter.

Grandma put on her spectacles and read the letter. Mum and Dad watched, as her face changed from curiosity to astonishment.

'Good heavens!' exclaimed Grandma. 'Oswald really means business, doesn't he? This is a huge sum of money.'

Mum, Dad and Grandma looked at one another, each feeling shaken.

'It's the sort of amount of money which few people turn down,' said Grandma, looking again at the letter. 'What are you going to do?'

Mum looked at Dad. Dad looked at the floor.

'I don't know,' he said, shaking his head. 'Living here is beyond a price – it is priceless. But, if we took Oswald's offer, we'd have enough money to buy a decent-sized house and not have to worry about school or university fees. We'd live very comfortably for the rest of our lives. It's a very seductive thought.'

'It's almost irresistible,' said Mum, thoughtfully. 'What a choice to have to make, eh?'

For a few moments, they were silent.

Then Mum said, 'I wonder if there is something behind it? I realise Oswald knows we'd have to be prised out of here kicking and screaming, so he'd have to make it a good offer – but this is ridiculous.'

'He must believe the land is worth it and that he'll make a lot of money,' said Dad. 'Property developers can be pretty ruthless.'

'The thought of Sprite Towers turned into a hotel and the garden covered in houses is heartbreaking,' said Mum, her big grey eyes sad and her bottom lip quivering. 'The girls would never forgive us.'

'No,' said Dad, taking her hand. 'But it would solve all of our financial issues.'

Mum nodded in agreement. They were silent again for

a moment, then Dad said. 'I think you should come up to the attics and look at the roof after lunch. It's in a pretty parlous state – and I'm not sure what to do.'

For the next half-hour, the three of them chatted over a lunch of cheese, home-grown salad and homemade bread and pickles. Dad told Mum and Grandma about the lost architectural commission.

'I'm so sorry, Colin,' said Grandma.

'There will be others, I'm sure,' said Mum. 'Didn't Stephen Glass mention something to you about a possible project at lunch on Sunday?'

'Yes,' said Dad. Then he picked up the letter, which had been lying on the table and looked at it again. 'I don't envisage ever being offered this amount of money in the rest of my life. It's a very strange feeling.'

'If things get desperate, perhaps we could sell some of the paintings?' suggested Mum.

'No, no!' said Dad, emphatically. 'We mustn't ever do that. Our portraits aren't high value art, but they mean a great deal to the family. We mustn't split up the collection. It's part of Sprite Towers.' He added wryly, 'Besides, Sidney Sprite would never forgive me.'

Mum and Grandma smiled.

'No, we'll have to find another way,' said Dad with a frown.

For a moment they sat there thinking about this, then they got up, cleared away the plates and climbed the wide mahogany staircase to the attics.

'By the way, did you call the builder, Colin?' asked Mum.

'Yes, he can't come round and have a look for the next two weeks, but he'll call as soon as he's free,' replied Dad.

He led Mum and Grandma to the end room at the east side of the house. Water trickled down the walls in several different rooms.

'This is bizarre,' said Mum, touching a wet wall. 'It hasn't rained for weeks. Where on earth is the water coming from?'

'That's what I wondered, when I was up here with the girls the other night,' said Dad.

'It feels as if we're under siege,' murmured Mum.

Grandma stared at the wall. We need a plan, she thought. We need to turn this dark magic around.

Glenda Glass's face flashed through her mind. She saw her thin nose and her sharp chin, the look of cold hatred in her rival's eyes.

Grandma raised her head high and pushed back her shoulders. In that instant, she looked like a warrior. Over my dead body, she thought. You are not having Sprite Towers, Glenda Glass – now or ever.

Then she said, suddenly, 'I know things look bad, but I believe you should think very carefully before responding to Oswald.'

Mum and Dad looked surprised.

'I'm sure the roof is mendable, Colin,' continued

Grandma. 'Our luck will change – I can feel it in my bones.'

'I hope so, Ma,' said Dad.

After their visit to the attics, Grandma went to her rooms on the first floor of the house. She had a large bedroom and a sitting room. The rooms were elegantly decorated with rose-patterned wallpaper and cream woodwork. She had a few pieces of fine furniture – a reminder of her wealthier days with her husband, Sheldon.

Marilyn Sprite had expected to be a widow with means, but life played a cruel trick on her.

When Colin and Ottalie moved to Sprite Towers after their marriage, Marilyn and Sheldon moved to the South of France. The warmer climate suited his health and they had many happy years there together. Sheldon transferred his business interests and got a French lawyer, whom he trusted. He assured his wife that she would be very comfortably off, if anything happened to him. She knew the lawyer, Pierre, reasonably well; they often met on social occasions. He had always seemed a nice man – and her husband was adamant that he was a good chap.

When Sheldon died, suddenly, it was Pierre who read out his will. This stated that Sheldon had left Sprite Towers to Colin, as Grandma knew he would, and that all the money was due to come to her.

She and Sheldon had agreed that when she passed away, the terms of *her* will would split the inheritance between

Colin and his younger sister, Anne. She had married an Australian and lived with her family in Sydney.

Then something very bizarre happened.

Within a week of Sheldon's death, just after the will had been read, Pierre the lawyer died, too. He had been a healthy man. His death – apparently from a heart attack – was sudden and unexpected.

Then, something even more bizarre happened.

In the depths of her grief, Marilyn Sprite found that her inheritance had vanished. Sheldon's bank account – which was about to be transferred to her own – had been emptied. The money had disappeared into thin air.

All she had left were a few savings in another bank.

There was uproar! Where on earth had the money gone to, everybody wondered?

The police and bank began to investigate. They suspected that Pierre had defrauded Marilyn Sprite of her inheritance in the days before his death and that, somehow, he had squirreled away the money – but, since he had died, no questions could be answered. The bank would not take responsibility for the fraud, until the case was proven. That was five years ago.

Despite everyone's efforts, the Sprites' money had never been found. It seemed that Pierre the lawyer had taken his secret to the grave. Grandma gave up hope of ever receiving her family's inheritance. With little means of financial support, she moved back to England and into Sprite

Towers with Colin and Ottalie and the girls, just after Flame's ninth birthday. Despite the ordeal and the sadness of losing Sheldon and all her money, she loved living with her family and they loved having her with them.

That afternoon, as the warm air blew in through the open window, Marilyn Sprite sat down at her pretty rosewood desk.

On top of the desk sat her computer. It was time to check her online investments.

She loved the cut and thrust of the financial markets. She might have lost her magical power, but she still had a sense as keen as a bat's sonar for which way the markets would move.

Since she had moved to Sprite Towers, she had proved a shrewd investor and had built up her small pile of capital into a tidy sum. It was not enough to repair the roof at Sprite Towers, but it was sufficient now to help out Colin and Ottalie, in the event of an emergency.

First, she checked her emails. There was one from Susan, an old friend still living in the South of France.

How nice to hear from her, thought Grandma.

Susan wrote to say that she had seen a piece in the local French newspaper about Sheldon's lawyer. The police had unearthed new information, she said. One thing the report mentioned was that Pierre had married only six months before his death.

I wonder why Pierre never mentioned his wife, thought

Grandma. Why would he have hidden her from us?

Susan wrote that an old friend of Pierre was quoted saying he'd been a decent chap until the last six months of his life. But, in that time before his death, Pierre became a changed man. He had become very secretive. It seemed not even his close friends knew of his marriage.

Then Pierre died unexpectedly. At the same time, his wife vanished and Sheldon Sprite's money disappeared. His wife's identity had been a mystery, as she had used a false name and papers.

Another thing, wrote Susan. *The police believe the wife was English. It was thought she'd gone to South America. I'll try and find out more.*

Grandma looked out of the window in front of her desk to the long, leafy driveway and the fields of ripening barley beyond.

I wonder if Pierre's wife has the money, she thought? Maybe she set him up from the start and Pierre did not realise. Why did he not want us to know about her? Or was it her? Was there something she did not want us to know?

For a few minutes, Grandma was lost in her memories. We were so happy, Sheldon and I, she thought. I still miss him . . .

She was about to check her online investments, when the email envelope symbol pinged again on the bottom of her screen.

It was another email from Susan.

I have just found out the wife's name, she wrote. *The police believe her surname is Frost. Does this ring any bells?*

Grandma stared at the screen in shock. She gaped at the name in disbelief.

Then she cried out, muffling the noise by putting her hand across her mouth.

Frost.

'No!' she cried. 'It can't be!'

Her mind began to race and whirr feverishly, but her body felt as cold as ice. Her fingers felt numb.

'*No!*' she said, with a moaning sound that came right from the bottom of her heart.

For a while, she sat there, head in her hands. Then she looked up and out of the window, out at the fields. She felt the breeze on her face.

Glenda.

Frost was her maiden name.

Grandma stood up, quickly, unable to bear the tension in her body. Inside, she felt as if she was screaming. She felt nauseous and swayed slightly, grabbing the edge of the desk to steady her. She heard her breath, jabbing, short and sharp. She felt the warm rosewood under her fingers. Her eyes moved restlessly around the room.

Somewhere deep, deep down in her heart, she *knew* that Glenda had been married to Pierre. The chances of this were a million to one, but Marilyn Sprite knew it was the truth. She knew her old rival well enough to know that it was the sort of thing Glenda would do.

She's a hard, scheming woman who will stop at nothing, she thought.

Anger moved through every part of her. She began to pace around her room – to the bed, to the window, to the desk. She could not stand still.

Why, she kept asking? *Why?*

Then, in a flash, she knew. It is not about me, she thought. This is about Sprite Towers. That's what Glenda is really after.

She stopped and leaned against the open window frame.

There's something in the house she wants – it's not just the house. It's something more than that . . .

We must not let her have it.

Keep calm. Think clearly . . .

Glenda Glass is my second cousin, she thought – a Sprite who broke the Sprite Code of Honour. She was my rival in the *corps de ballet* and she was my rival in love.

And now, she thought, gazing out at the swaying barley in the fields beyond the garden wall, she has my money. And with it she wants to buy our house.

The irony. The supreme irony . . .

The anger began to rise again.

There's not a shred of decency in that woman, she thought. Not a shred.

Grandma felt so upset that she left her room, walked quickly downstairs and went out to the Rose Garden.

There, for the next half-hour, she weeded the flowerbeds, furiously jabbing the dry soil with her trowel.

She was not a woman given to tears, but that afternoon, she cried and cried. Through the tears, Grandma's strength and resolve came roaring back.

We are not letting Glenda take Sprite Towers from us, she decided. I don't care how much money she has told Oswald to offer us. They will have to carry me out of this house in a wooden box before I let her in here ever again.

Mum was in the conservatory as Grandma rushed out to the Rose Garden. She noticed her tense face and wondered whether to go out and ask what was the matter, but then decided to let her be.

She left her for half an hour, then carried two mugs of tea out to the Rose Garden.

Grandma looked up from the rose bed, wiped her eyes with the back of her hand and smiled at Mum's kind face.

'Thanks, love,' she said, standing up and taking the mug.

Mum looked at Grandma's tear-streaked face and waited.

'I had an email from Susan in France,' said Grandma.

'Oh,' replied Mum. They moved to the wooden bench and sat down.

'You remember our lawyer, Pierre?'

'The one who stole the family money?'

'Yes, him.'

Mum waited, as Grandma seemed to grapple with her emotions.

'Apparently, he married six months before he died,' said Grandma, taking a mouthful of tea from her mug.

'Didn't you know?' asked Mum.

'No, nobody did.' Grandma looked into Mum's clear grey eyes. Mum waited.

'It seems his wife's surname was Frost.'

Mum looked baffled – but waited.

'That was the maiden name of Glenda Glass. I am *certain* that she was Pierre's wife.'

Mum nearly dropped her mug of tea. 'You mean *Stephen's mother*? *Verena's grandmother*?'

Grandma nodded.

Mum's face was incredulous. 'I'm – I'm . . . It's – it's *incredible!*'

'Yes,' agreed Grandma quietly.

They were silent for a moment, as Mum thought about this.

Then Grandma said, 'I think she may have our money.'

Mum's face went white. 'How?' she whispered.

'I don't know,' replied Grandma.

'Are the police still investigating?'

'I believe so,' replied Grandma.

Mum stared at the roses, oblivious of everything but the information that she had learned.

'Frost is not an uncommon name,' she said, trying to

make sense of it all. 'There must be many women named that. How are you so sure it's her?'

'I know,' agreed Grandma. 'I know it seems incredible – but I feel, deep inside, that it's her – the Glenda we know. I think she may be behind Oswald's offer.'

'But *why*?'

'Because she's a Sprite and she wants Sprite Towers,' said Grandma.

'Then she must not have it!' said Mum, firmly. 'We must not sell it! We must talk with Colin. We must find a way!'

Dad's first reaction was to doubt his mother's explanation.

'There are lots of Frosts,' he said. 'And besides, the police are not sure of this woman's surname. It could be anybody, Mother.'

When he looked into his mother's eyes, however, he knew instinctively that she was right. In all his life, he had learned never to doubt his mother's deep feelings. She was a wise and intelligent woman and if she knew something deep in her heart, it was always true.

Then he exploded, livid with rage.

He strode around the Rose Garden with his long-legged strides and waved his arms. 'It's OUTRAGEOUS!' he shouted. 'Oswald is offering to buy OUR house with OUR money! No wonder he made us such a big offer!'

He made a big roaring noise and took off round the huge

rolling lawn, clenching his fists. 'I feel like pummelling Oswald's smarmy face with a knuckle sandwich! Argh!'

A few minutes later, when Dad had let off steam, they all sat down again in the Rose Garden.

'I realise there's a long way to go to prove this in a Court of Law, and that we may not find the money – *and* that we don't know for sure,' said Grandma. 'But I do have a strong feeling about it.'

'Well, as Ottalie says, we must not sell,' said Dad. 'We must not. We have to find a way.'

'I don't suppose Oswald has a clue about Glenda's real character, or where the money came from,' said Grandma. 'I'll bet she is one of his company's directors – that's why he can offer you such a huge amount of money to buy Sprite Towers.'

'And Verena?' said Mum, softly. 'What about her?'

She looked at Dad and Grandma anxiously. 'Do you think she is OK?'

'I hope so, poor girl,' said Dad. 'Shall I say something to Stephen? We may see him at Speech Day tomorrow.'

'What can you say?' smiled Mum, ironically. 'Stephen, old chap, I believe your mother is a thief?'

Dad smiled, wanly. 'Hmm, probably not a good idea.'

They were silent for a moment.

'It does fit with the fact that Verena didn't know her grandmother until recently,' said Mum. 'People say she lived in South America, before she came here.'

'South America!' cried Grandma. 'That's where Pierre's wife was supposed to have gone!'

'I wonder what really happened to Pierre?' said Dad, staring up at the sky.

'Goodness – you're not suggesting that anything untoward happened to him, are you?' said Mum.

'Well, I don't know,' he replied. 'It is all very strange.' Then he looked at Grandma and asked, 'What do you think, Ma?'

'It wouldn't surprise me if Pierre met a sticky end,' she said. 'I knew Glenda years ago to be a ruthless woman.'

'That doesn't necessarily make her a murderer!' said Dad.

'Come on, we don't know *what* happened to Pierre,' interrupted Mum.

'No, we don't,' agreed Dad. 'But I would like to know what happened to our family money – and I'm sure we'd all like it back.'

Grandma was silent, absorbed in this thought. She stared at a perfectly formed pink rosebud.

'Verena is leaving to see her mother the day after tomorrow,' said Mum.

This information hung in the air. Then she added, thoughtfully, 'I wonder if Glenda had anything to do with Zoe's sudden departure?'

Dad looked at her, quizzically. 'Stephen was very surprised when she took off to Buenos Aires so suddenly,' he said. 'He says he still loves her and wants her to come home.'

'I wonder if all is as it seems?' said Mum.

'Probably not,' said Dad.

'Shall we tell the girls?'

'I don't think we should say anything to them or anyone else, until there's some proof,' said Dad.

Then he turned to Grandma, who was still looking at the rosebud, deep in thought, and said, 'Are you *really* sure it is Glenda, Ma?'

Grandma looked deep into his warm brown eyes. 'Yes, love. I can feel it in my bones.

'Hmm,' said Dad, stroking his chin.

'Trust me,' said Grandma.

For the next minute they were silent, each absorbed in their own thoughts.

Then Dad said, resolutely, 'Well, we must mend the roof and keep Sprite Towers. I don't how we'll do it, but we must find a way.'

His words hung in the air.

'Yes,' agreed Mum.

'We *will* find a way,' said Grandma.

'Oh, goodness – I'm late for the girls!' said Mum, looking at her watch, and she rushed off to collect them.

Half an hour later, the Sprite Sisters burst into the house, whooping and happy. One more day at school, then it would be the summer holidays – seven weeks in which to run around the garden and woods and fields. Seven weeks in which to relax and have fun.

After they had eaten large pieces of Grandma's home-made banana bread and drunk glasses of her special lemonade, they got on their bicycles and raced around the grounds. They tore down the driveway, then up around the big field and over the huge rolling lawn. For the first time in two weeks, Flame and Marina laughed together as if nothing had happened.

And that evening, while Mum and Grandma cooked the supper and Dad went down to the vegetable garden, the Sprite Sisters went up to the attics. There, they started to mend part of the roof using their magic powers – and they mended it well.

On the bit that they mended together, the water stopped trickling. The wall dried out and the attic suddenly seemed like the place they loved and remembered.

'We can relax,' said Marina, smiling, as they heard Grandma call them down for supper.

'Yes,' said Flame, but as she said the word she could hear another warning bell ringing somewhere deep down in her mind.

CHAPTER ELEVEN

✳

THE SECRET IN THE CUPBOARDS

✳

THE LAST day of the summer term dawned bright and fair. The Sprite Sisters got up and put on their freshly laundered school dresses and polished shoes and ate a hearty breakfast. Then Dad drove them to school and came home.

An hour later, he and Mum left the house wearing their smartest clothes, got into the big red car and drove to school.

It was Thursday, 5th July and Drysdale's Speech Day.

This was the day when the schoolmasters and mistresses put on their long black gowns and mortarboards, the pupils put on their school blazers and everyone shone their shoes.

The Quad was bustling with people when Mum and

Dad drove in. Hundreds of parents were walking towards the school hall.

'There you are, girls!' said Mum, as the Sprite Sisters bounced up.

A moment later, Verena came up to Mum.

'Daddy couldn't come,' she said, sadly. 'Again.'

'Oh, Verena, I'm so sorry,' said Mum. She put her arm around Verena's shoulder.

'I'm really looking forward to seeing Mummy,' said Verena.

'Yes, you must be,' said Mum. 'And I'm sure she is really looking forward to seeing you, dear. I hope you have a lovely time with her. Please give her our love. When do you leave?'

'Tomorrow morning,' said Verena. She looked behind her. 'Grandma is here – so is Uncle Oswald. He pretends to come for me, but I know it's because he can do some business and network.'

'Oh,' said Mum – then saw them approaching. Glenda looked tall and elegant in a cream linen suit. Oswald wore his crocodile shoes.

As she looked at Glenda Glass, Mum's face seemed to turn to stone. It was the stoniest look she had ever given anybody in the whole of her life. In fact, it was so stony that Glenda hesitated for a second, then turned to talk to someone passing.

Verena looked at Mum in disbelief. Even the Sprite Sisters looked surprised.

Seeing Glenda turn, Mum breathed out and smiled.

'Well come on, girls,' she said. 'Let's go in.'

'Well done,' said Dad, under his breath.

Oswald, however, was oblivious of everything and smarmed up to Dad. 'Did you get the letter, old chap?'

'Yes, Oswald, we did.'

'And?'

'The answer is still the same,' said Dad, looking Oswald in the eye.

'What? You are going to turn down all that money!' Oswald looked incredulous. 'Are you *mad*?'

'Yep, 'fraid so,' said Dad and turned away.

For a moment, Oswald looked as if someone had hit him over the head, but he was a consummate performer and soon recovered his oily charm. 'You'll never get such a good offer from anyone else!' he said to Dad's back. 'I'll ring you over the weekend – I'm sure you'll have changed your mind by then.'

Glenda caught up with Oswald and they followed a little way behind the Sprites and Verena. Oswald whispered to her, clearly flustered, but Glenda remained cool and aloof. She had one ear on him, but the other on Ottalie Sprite and Verena, who were walking together a little way in front.

Verena turned and said to Mum, 'By the way, Daddy says he'll see you at the wedding on Saturday.'

'Oh, he's coming – good!' said Mum, smiling at Verena. Their words reached Glenda.

Ah, she thought, the parents are leaving Sprite Towers . . .

* * *

Drysdale's Speech Day was a splendid affair. The school governors and staff sat on the stage. The prefects sat behind them. Trophies, prizes and badges were handed out and the Sprite Sisters got their fair share. Batty Blenkinsop summed up the school year and talked of how proud the school was to win the National Schools Music Competition. When he thanked the school's musicians, singers and teachers, everyone clapped. There was an interesting speech by the guest speaker, a famous lady scientist; then a short speech by the head of the school governors and another by the head boy. After this, there were the art exhibition, various musical and dramatic performances – and lunch.

Meanwhile, back at Sprite Towers, Grandma and Mrs Duggery were deep inside a large cupboard in the attics. Only two people were allowed to attend Drysdale's Speech Day, owing to the pressure of seats in the hall, so Grandma did not go – but she did not mind. She had been to many speech days in her life. Besides, she enjoyed talking to Mrs Duggery about Sprite Towers and how things used to be and was glad to have some help sorting out the cupboards.

Grandma hated clutter. She liked to get rid of things that were not being used. She had wanted to turn out the cupboards for a long time, but could not do this on her own. Mum and Dad were too busy with their family and work to spend time clearing out cupboards.

Now, for the last few days, she'd had the help of Mrs

Duggery. Together the two women had worked through all the cupboards in the house.

Today, they were on the final cupboard – a big cupboard, several metres deep and about two metres wide, at the west end of the corridor, by the tower door. Grandma and Mrs Duggery carried each item or together lifted each piece of furniture out into the corridor and assessed it. If it looked useful, they put it on the left side of the corridor: the 'keep it' side. If it did not look useful, then they put it on the right, to be given away or sent to the auction house to be sold. There were far more pieces of furniture on the right-hand side – along with vases and mirrors, several commodes and a brass gong.

'I had no idea we had quite so much old junk up here,' said Grandma, as they carried out the final piece of furniture – yet another very ordinary gateleg table.

The cupboard was full of cobwebs. Grandma was dressed in jeans and an old pink shirt and had tied a headscarf over her hair. Her face was streaked with dust. Mrs Duggery wore her knitted hat and an apron and looked pretty dusty, too.

'Is that it – everything out?' Grandma called to Mrs Duggery, who was now standing right at the back of the cupboard and was about to sweep it out.

'Come an' look here, Marilyn,' called the tiny old lady.

'What is it?' said Grandma standing in the open doorway, peering into the dark.

'There's summat on the wall here,' said Mrs Duggery,

staring in front of her.

'It's so dark – how can you see anything properly?'

'I can see all right,' said Mrs Duggery. 'But you'll see better if you bring in the torch.'

Grandma found the torch they'd been using, switched it on and took it into the cupboard.

'Point it up here,' said Mrs Duggery, touching the wall above her. This was at Grandma's eye level.

Grandma stared at the wall, shining in the beam of light. 'It looks like a hand print in the plaster,' she said. 'A man's hand – a man's right hand.'

She touched the wall and ran her hand over the shape. 'I can feel the depression made by the fingers and palm – it must have been made when the plaster was wet.'

Mrs Duggery nodded. 'Hmm,' she said and pointed up. 'Look what's round the side of it.'

Grandma ran the torch beam in a circle around the hand, then stopped and moved it in the shape of a square. Then she held the torch still and ran her hand over the plaster again.

'There seems to be a line around the hand – in the plaster. It's not drawn on. I can feel it cut in.'

'Hmm,' agreed Mrs Duggery. 'Thas what I thought.'

'What do you think it is?' asked Grandma.

'I think thas one a Sidney Sprite's signs. Yes, thas what it is.' Mrs Duggery nodded to herself.

'What – part of the magic he built into the house?'

'Yes,' Mrs Duggery stretched up her right arm and

placed her tiny right hand on the hand print in the wall.

Grandma had no idea what would happen – but she did not expect to see the hand print light up with an eerie blue glow.

'Good gracious!' she exclaimed. 'The wall lit up around your hand!'

Mrs Duggery smiled and took her hand away. 'Now you try,' she said.

Grandma raised her right hand and was about to place it on the wall – but hesitated.

'I don't think it will work for me,' she said, lowering her hand. 'My power went a long time ago.'

'Come on, Marilyn dear, jus' try,' said Mrs Duggery. 'Have faith.'

Grandma looked at the wall. It was over forty years since she had last used her magic power. It disappeared after the night she fought Glenda Glass on the dark street. She had never felt it again.

Mrs Duggery waited. Grandma lifted her hand and slowly and carefully placed it over the hand print.

Nothing happened. She took her hand down quickly.

'I thought so,' she said. A look of sadness passed over her face.

'Try again,' said Mrs Duggery, taking Grandma's hand and lifting it up. '*Come on.*'

Grandma sighed.

'You need ter *believe* it,' said Mrs Duggery, with warmth

in her old voice.

Grandma nodded. Then she raised her hand again and placed it on the hand print.

'Close yer eyes an' *feel* it,' said Mrs Duggery.

Grandma closed her eyes and waited.

'Oh!' she said, suddenly. 'Oh my goodness!'

As the ripple of energy whooshed through her hand, a faint blue light shone like a halo around it.

'I'd forgotten what it feels like,' said Grandma, staring at the back of her hand.

'There yer go,' said Mrs Duggery. 'Yer power int gone.'

Grandma took her hand off the wall and stared at her palm. She wiggled her fingers. A tear ran down her dusty cheek, but she was laughing at the same time.

'You did well,' said Mrs Duggery.

'Thank you, Violet.'

Mrs Duggery reached up and put her tiny arm around Grandma's shoulders.

'Come on, my dear, let's go an' have a cuppa tea. Time for one of them chocolate biscuits.'

The warm July sunshine shone into the kitchen. On the kitchen table was a huge jug full of flowers from the garden. Bert lay sprawled by the open door in a sausage-doggy heap. Pudding sat on the Windsor chair, licking his grey and black paws.

'I wonder why we found the hand print at this time?'

mused Grandma, leaning on the table, holding her mug of tea.

'Thas time for the magic in the house ter wake up,' said Mrs Duggery. 'Thas a sign that things need attention.'

'Such as the roof?'

'Exactly,' replied Mrs Duggery.

'Shall we tell the girls?'

Mrs Duggery picked up her fourth chocolate biscuit from the plate. 'Yes – Sidney wants 'em to strengthen their magic.'

Grandma put down her mug of tea and looked at Mrs Duggery. 'Who *knew* about Sidney's magic?'

'I int sure if his brothers were aware, but each of Sidney's three sisters knew about it,' said Mrs Duggery. 'Yer grandmother, Alice, an' he were very close. She were a lovely woman and had good magic. Then there were my mother, Elisa, the youngest 'on 'em six children – she had good strong magic. Margaret, Sidney's older sister – Glenda's grandmother – she 'ad a lot a power, too, but as you know, she went bad. She became very jealous of Sidney an' started to use her power against him an' his family. In the end, he turned her out of Sprite Towers and forbade her to enter the house again. That part of the family went bad.'

Mrs Duggery chewed her fifth biscuit thoughtfully.

'But they didn't *all* go bad in that line of the family,' said Grandma. 'Stephen Glass, Glenda's son, is charming and a good man. And Verena – I believe there is good in her, though I suspect she can be manipulative.'

'Yes, thas funny 'ow some on 'em are good and some are bad, and some have the power and others don't,' said Mrs Duggery.

'Yes,' Grandma agreed.

By the time that Mum and Dad and the Sprite Sisters arrived back that afternoon, Grandma had showered and changed her clothes and Mrs Duggery had cycled off on her old boneshaker bicycle.

Grandma greeted each of the girls with a hug. Then the whole family went up to the attics, to see the furniture that she and Mrs Duggery had cleared out.

Dad opened the cupboard door and looked into the empty dark space. Then he turned to look at the furniture piled up in the corridor.

'Blimey!' he said. 'You say all that came from in here, Ma? It doesn't seem possible!'

'Yes, all that was in here.' Grandma stared at the furniture. 'I'd like you and Ottalie to check it, please. I've ordered the van to collect this lot tomorrow.'

She pointed at the huge amount of furniture and junk that lay on the right side of the corridor. There were only three things on the left side which she deemed worthy of being kept.

'Right-ho,' said Dad, rubbing his hands together with delight. 'Oh look, there's a gong!'

'Colin, please don't start saying we need any of this

stuff!' said Mum, aware that, now Dad had seen all these things he did not know he had, he might start to want them.

Dad was a magpie: he loved to collect things. To him, everything was potentially useful.

'Oh, but I really think we should keep the gong, Ottalie!' he protested.

'We already *have* a gong – a much nicer gong than that!' exclaimed Mum.

'But it could go in my office,' said Dad. 'I could use it to summon you, when I wanted a cup of tea.'

The Sprite Sisters giggled.

'No, Colin, the gong is going to the auction house,' said Mum, getting flustered.

She threw Ash a look that said, 'Help'.

Ash knew the best way to divert her father's attention. 'Dad,' she said, taking his arm.

'What, love?' he replied, peering underneath a gateleg table.

'Can we go down to the vegetable garden, please?' said Ash. 'It would be nice to be quiet after such a busy day and there are a lot of raspberries to pick for supper.'

Dad was immediately distracted. 'Of course,' he said. He stood up and looked round at the pile of furniture with a wistful expression.

Mum looked at him with a face that said, 'I'll deal with this.'

'Okay, Ash – lead on,' said Dad. As he followed her

downstairs, Mum and Grandma breathed a sigh of relief. Flame, Marina and Ariel giggled.

Grandma herded the girls back down – she did not want them to find the hand print. If they had any hint of magic in the cupboard, they would immediately start to explore.

Tomorrow morning she would tell them about it – then Mrs Duggery would explain what it all meant. That was the way she planned it.

Once the furniture was sorted, Mum and Grandma went downstairs to the kitchen. As soon as Flame, Marina and Ariel knew they had gone, they ran back up to the attics.

Flame opened the cupboard door wide. They all walked in.

'It's ever so dark in here,' said Ariel, peering round.

'Just wait a moment – your eyes will adjust,' said Flame.

Marina walked to the far wall and touched it. 'It smells really musty,' she said.

'Well, I don't s'pose anybody's been in here for years,' said Flame. 'We never come in here – it's always been piled high with stuff. It's probably been like that since the house was built. I'll bet Sidney liked to collect things – it's probably where Dad gets it from.'

'He does,' agreed Ariel. 'Sidney told me so.'

Marina and Flame laughed. They had often seen their little sister standing in front of Sidney Sprite's portrait, at the bottom of the staircase.

'What do you and Sidney talk about?' asked Marina.

'All sorts of things,' said Ariel, pointing her ski-jump nose in the air.

'Such as?'

'Such as – there's magic in this cupboard,' said Ariel, authoritatively.

'Where?' asked Marina.

The three sisters peered round the walls.

'There is something in here – I can sense it,' said Flame.

'So can I,' said Marina.

'What's this, up here?' said Ariel, standing at the back of the cupboard. 'It looks like a hand.'

Flame and Marina moved beside her. Flame stretched out her hand and ran it over the wall, just as Grandma had done a few hours earlier.

As she felt her way over the print, she said, 'It seems to be a hand print, set into the plaster. There's a depression on the surface of the wall.'

'Let me have a feel,' said Marina and she felt the wall.

'You're right,' she said. Then she ran her fingers around the hand print in an arc.

'There's a square shape round it in the plaster,' she said.

'I wonder if there's something behind here,' said Flame.

'That would be so cool!' said Ariel. 'Let me have a feel.'

Ariel reached up and ran her stubby pink hand over the wall. As she did so, she shut her eyes and bit her lip.

'There's . . . there's . . . '

'What?' asked Marina. 'What is it?'

'It's like a space behind it,' said Ariel. 'But there's something in the space.'

'We mustn't do this without Ash here,' said Flame.

Ariel lowered her hand and blinked. 'That was a bit strange,' she said.

'What do you think it is?' asked Marina.

Ariel stared at her fingers and wiggled them. 'I don't know, but it's made my fingers go all tingly.'

As soon as the sisters walked through the kitchen, Grandma knew they had found the hand print. Their faces gave it away. But, since Mum was standing there, she could not say anything. Flame, Marina and Ariel knew that Grandma had them sussed. Her face said to them, 'I know exactly what you are up to and I want you to leave the cupboard alone!'

They smiled at Grandma and walked out through the kitchen door. Then they ran over the huge rolling lawn to the vegetable garden.

Ash was picking raspberries. 'You coming to help?' she asked her sisters, seeing them standing there.

'Jolly good, girls – grab a bowl!' said Dad.

'What's up?' Ash whispered to Marina when they didn't move.

'We've found something in the cupboard,' Marina whispered back.

Dad was humming away as he leaned into the raspberry bushes and picked the fat red fruits.

'That'll do,' he said. 'We've got enough raspberries now – but we could pick some spinach, Ash. And I think we'd better cut some of those lettuces.'

'Okey doke, Dad,' she replied. Then she turned to Flame and whispered, 'Let's look tonight.'

Flame nodded and a moment later she, Marina and Ariel sped off to move the rabbit and guinea pig cages on the lawn and top up the water supplies.

'Leave the cupboard till tomorrow,' said Grandma, as she said goodnight to Flame later that evening. 'We'll look with Mrs Duggery. I somehow think that will be best.'

Flame nodded. 'Night, Grandma.'

Flame, Marina, Ash and Ariel lay in their beds. It was a clear night and moonlight poured in through their bedroom curtains. By midnight, when Mum and Dad and Grandma had settled in their rooms, not one of the Sprite Sisters was asleep. They lay in their beds, waiting.

Then, as everything became still, they crept up the attic staircase, quiet as mice, and tiptoed along the corridor to the cupboard.

Flame carried a small torch, which she kept in her room.

The four Sprite Sisters stood in front of the cupboard. Flame opened the door and pointed the torch into the gloomy space. She held the beam steady, as they all walked forward into the dark.

All they could hear was the sound of their breathing.

'You better close the door, Marina,' Flame said to her sister.

Marina pulled the door until it was only slightly ajar.

Apart from the light of Flame's torch, they were in pitch black. Flame ran the beam over the wall until she found the hand print. The four sisters moved towards it.

They stared, silent, at the hand print caught in the narrow beam of light.

'It's Sidney's hand print,' whispered Ariel in her breathy voice. 'He told me to look for it.'

'I think we should touch it,' whispered Flame.

'Yes. You go first,' said Marina. 'I'll hold the torch.'

Flame laid her long, slim hand on the hand print, closed her eyes and focused her mind. Almost instantly, an eerie blue glow appeared around her hand.

'Wow,' she said, jerking her hand back. 'The power is very strong.'

She took the torch from Marina, who held up her hand and did the same. 'Yes, it is!' As the blue light burst out, she pulled her hand back, too.

Then Ash had a turn. The same thing happened again. She stared at her hand afterwards and wiggled her fingers.

Last was Ariel. She breathed heavily as she held up her hand. The eerie blue light lit up suddenly.

'Ow!' she squeaked, pulling her hand away.

'Sssh!' whispered her older sisters.

The blue light faded.

'Are you all right?' Ash whispered to Ariel.

'Yes, it's made my fingers feel all funny. Are you okay?'

'My fingers feel funny, too.'

Flame held the beam of light on the hand print.

'There's definitely something behind here,' she whispered.

'What shall we do?' whispered Ash.

'How about we all put our hands on the hand print at the same time?' suggested Marina, in a low whisper.

'Good idea,' agreed Flame, softly. For a second she stared at the wall. 'I hope this is safe. I'd better go first,' she said. Then, with the torch in her left hand, she placed her right hand on the hand print on the wall.

'I bring the power of Fire,' she whispered. As her hand made contact, the eerie blue light shone out again.

Then Marina held up her hand and placed it over Flame's. 'I bring the power of Water,' she said. The blue light glowed stronger.

'Hey!' said Marina, softly. 'Look at *that*!'

Then it was Ash's turn. 'Earth,' she said, as she placed her hand on top of Marina's. The blue light grew stronger still. The wall around the hand print lit up in a dazzling blue glow.

'Now you, pumpkin,' said Marina to Ariel.

Ariel's big grey eyes were as wide as saucers as she placed her hand on top of Ash's.

'I bring the power of Air,' she whispered.

There was a flash of brilliant blue light and a loud crack.

'AHH!' gasped the Sprite Sisters, jerking back their hands. 'What was that?'

'*Shhh!*' whispered Flame.

They stared at the wall – then gasped again, as the square line deepened around the hand print. The cream plaster started to crack.

The eerie blue light began to glow once more, pulsing in waves.

'What is it?' whispered Flame.

The square shape was now clearly visible on the wall.

'I think it's a door!' said Ash. 'Look!'

Sure enough, the piece of wall within the square line moved backwards.

The Sprite Sisters jumped back. Flame nearly dropped the torch.

'*Shhh!*' hissed Ash. Then she whispered, 'Keep calm.'

Once more, Flame pointed the torch at the wall. They waited, their hearts beating fast.

The blue light was getting stronger and stronger. Then, just as it was almost too bright to look at, it dimmed, and what looked like a little square door creaked open.

The Sprite Sisters waited, silent, breathing fast.

With her heart beating so hard she could hardly think, Flame reached out to touch the little square door.

Whatever lay behind it emanated a blue light that pulsed in waves.

The Sprite Sisters stared in silence as Flame opened the

little door wide, to show a small recess cut into the wall – a tiny cupboard within a big cupboard.

'What is it?' whispered Ariel, but before she had finished speaking, the blue light dimmed, very suddenly – and then went out.

The Sprite Sisters gulped. Flame shone the torch. Lying on the bottom of the recess was a small round object.

'It looks like a stone,' said Flame, pointing the torch as steadily as she could.

'What shall we do?' asked Ash.

'Grandma said we weren't to touch the cupboard,' whispered Flame. 'I think we should leave it. Mrs Duggery will know what to do.'

Ash stared at the stone. 'I have the power of Earth – and a stone is part of the earth. I'd like to hold it.' And before Flame could stop her, she reached into the cupboard and took it in her hand.

By the light of the torch, the Sprite Sisters looked at the grey-brown stone lying on Ash's outstretched palm. It covered the palm of her hand and was round in shape, with two flattened sides. Ash turned it in her fingers, feeling its smoothness.

'Look, it's got black lines running through it,' she whispered. 'Isn't it meant to be lucky if lines go all the way round a stone?'

She handed it to Flame, who held it for a minute then passed it to Marina. She in turn, passed it to Ariel.

Then Ash held out her hand, 'I'll take it,' she said to Ariel. 'We'll ask Mrs Duggery about it tomorrow.'

'Where will you keep it?' asked Flame. 'How do we know it won't hurt you?'

Ash stared at the stone. 'I have the power of Earth. It won't hurt me,' she said. 'I think it has come to help us.'

'With the roof?' asked Ariel.

Ash nodded and looked at Flame.

In that instant, the tall copper-haired girl had the flash of Glenda's face in her mind, but she said nothing about it. 'Yes,' she agreed, quietly. 'The roof.'

The Sprite Sisters were not the only people to be aware of the magic stone, that night.

As Mrs Duggery ate her last chocolate biscuit in the light of the moon, in her mind she saw the girls standing in the cupboard and Ash holding a stone in her hand.

The power in Sprite Towers is waking up, she thought. The girls have awakened it.

Downstairs in her bedroom on the first floor at Sprite Towers, Grandma dreamed of Sidney Sprite and saw him handing Ash a smooth grey-brown stone.

And, at The Oaks, Glenda Glass woke up with a start and sat up in bed.

They have new power, she thought. I can feel it. But not for long . . .

Then she flopped back down on the pillow.

* * *

Ash got into bed. She held the magic stone on her flat, open hand. A ray of moonlight fell on her bed, through the slit in the curtains. Ash held the stone in the silver light and watched it.

She smiled, turning the stone in her hand, marvelling at its smoothness.

'Thank you for sending the magic stone, Sidney,' she smiled. Then she put it under her pillow, shut her eyes and fell into a deep sleep.

In the attic cupboard, the little square door swung shut. Then, silently, the cream plaster on the wall repaired itself. The cracks disappeared. The hand print smoothed out and that, too, disappeared.

If anyone opened the cupboard door and looked in now, all they would see was a cream wall.

CHAPTER TWELVE

✳

THE LULL BEFORE THE STORM

✳ ✳

✳

As soon as Ariel woke on Friday morning, she went through to Ash's room and climbed into bed beside her. The two sisters lay there, looking at the magic stone.

'I wonder what's going to happen?' said Ariel, holding the stone in the air. 'Do you think it means we'll have to use lots of magic this summer?'

Ash grinned. 'Hope so.'

'When I touched the stone, it was a different feeling from when I usually use my magic power,' said Ariel. 'Was it the same for you?'

'Yes – it felt very strong. So strong that I wasn't sure I

could control it.' Ash took the stone from her sister and held it up, turning it round and round.

'It looks like any old stone, doesn't it?' said Ariel. 'Nobody would know it's magic.'

'I think that's why most people don't see magic,' said Ash. 'They're too busy looking for something unusual. There is magic all around us, only people don't realise.'

The door opened and in came Marina, in her spotty pyjamas. Her thick, curly hair sprawled on her shoulders.

'Morning,' she said, flopping down on the bed. Ash handed her the stone. Marina pushed her hair away from her face and yawned, all the time looking at the stone. Then she looked at her two younger sisters – Ash with her tufty chestnut-brown hair and warm brown eyes and Ariel with her big grey eyes and fluffy blond hair.

'Look at you two!' she laughed.

'What?' said Ash and Ariel, together.

'You look so sweet lying there – like two little angels.'

'We are little angels,' said Ariel, trying to point her nose in the air, which was difficult lying down.

'Yeah, right!' laughed Marina. Ash and Ariel giggled.

Marina turned the smooth stone in her hand.

The door opened again. 'There you are,' said Flame. Marina moved up the bed and Flame sat down, crossing her long legs underneath her.

Marina handed her the stone. 'We ought to tell Grandma.'

'Yes, we will,' agreed Flame. She ran her finger over the

criss-cross of lines that ran around the stone.

'If Grandma looks in the cupboard, she'll see the little door in the wall and know we've been in there,' said Ash.

'No, she won't,' said Flame, with a mysterious smile.

'What do you mean?' asked Marina.

'I just went to check the cupboard: the little door has disappeared and so has the hand print.'

'Weird,' said Ash, sitting up.

'Really?' exclaimed Marina.

'Hmm,' agreed Flame, yawning. She covered her mouth with her hand.

'Do you think the stone will give us more power to mend the roof?' asked Marina.

'Yes, I expect so.' Flame looked at the round, brown-grey stone. 'It's got wonderful lines through it. Look – there's a big circle, with two lines crossing it.'

The Sprite Sisters were so absorbed, that they did not hear Grandma walk into the room.

'Good morning, girls,' she said, suddenly.

The Sprite Sisters jumped.

'Grandma!' they exclaimed.

Grandma held out her hand. 'Show me, please.'

Flame handed her the stone. Just as they had done, Grandma turned it and ran her fingers over its smooth surface.

Ariel sat up. Marina and Flame moved up the bed and Grandma sat down. She was wearing a long, pale-blue dressing gown and looked elegant even at this time of the day.

'We must show it to Mrs Duggery,' she said, holding the stone in front of her. 'There is a reason it has come into your lives now. Nothing happens by chance, as I always tell you.'

She stared thoughtfully at the stone, turning it over and over. 'It's here to protect you,' she said.

Flame watched her grandmother. Then she said, 'We put our hands over the hand print on the wall, Grandma. This little door opened and behind it was a recess – like a tiny cupboard – and this amazing blue light. Then the light disappeared – and we saw the stone.' Her face shone as she described it.

'I *knew* you wouldn't be able to resist going up to the cupboard, despite my telling you not to,' said Grandma, shaking her head.

The Sprite Sisters lowered their heads. 'Sorry, Grandma,' they all said.

'I understand it's tempting, but just be careful – *please*.'

After breakfast on the first day of the summer holidays, Dad went off to the office and Mum gave a piano lesson in the dining room. Mrs Duggery and Grandma climbed the wide mahogany staircase to the attics and sat down on two old armchairs, side by side, amidst the pile of junk and old furniture in the corridor. Marina and Ariel sat on the arms of the chairs. Ash and Flame sat on the floor in front of them.

Ash handed the magic stone to the tiny lady. It fitted neatly into her palm. Immediately, it emanated a bright blue light. The girls' faces lit up with delight. Mrs Duggery smiled.

'What do you think, Mrs Duggery?' asked Flame.

'I don' think – I *know*,' replied Mrs Duggery, looking at the stone.

Flame blinked, worried that she had offended Mrs Duggery, but the old lady smiled a twinkly smile.

'You'll know what I mean in time,' she said. 'There's a difference.'

Flame was curious. 'How?'

'Most people say, "I think this" or "I believe tha",' said Mrs Duggery. 'The important thing is ter know summat, not just ter believe it.'

'How does a person *know* things?'

'By openin' yer heart an' mind – and trustin' your instinct, thas how,' said Mrs Duggery. 'That takes patience.'

Flame smiled. 'Thank you,' she said.

'Now this here stone,' continued Mrs Duggery. 'Thas come to help you.'

The Sprite Sisters were alert and attentive.

'Sidney Sprite built magic into Sprite Towers. He wants you ter find it an' use it.' Mrs Duggery looked round at each of the four sisters in turn, then said, 'There are battles ahead an' wrongs ter be righted. You'll need the power in the house an' garden if yer ter succeed. This stone will lead you ter find it. It will also help you ter strengthen your own unique power – the powers of Fire, Water, Earth and Air. These powers need to be balanced for the magic to be strong. Everything you need is 'ere, somewhere, within the house and grounds of

Sprite Towers. The stone'll guide you – and it'll *warn* you. You mus' learn ter discern what thas tellin' you.'

The Sprite Sisters watched and listened to the old woman in the lilac knitted hat as they had never watched or listened to anyone before – even Grandma or their parents. Their hearts were pounding and their minds focused.

Mrs Duggery looked into Flame's clear green eyes. 'Go ter the East, Flame, ter find the power of Fire an' the gift of the human spirit an' inspiration.'

Flame nodded, silent.

Mrs Duggery looked into Marina's bright blue eyes. 'Go ter the South, Marina, ter find the power of Water an' the gift of feelings.'

'Yes,' said Marina, very quietly.

Mrs Duggery turned to Ash and looked into her warm brown eyes. 'Go ter the West, Ash, ter find the power of Earth and the human body's material needs. Learn how to look deep in ter yerself.'

Ash nodded, then breathed out a long, long breath.

Mrs Duggery looked into Ariel's big grey eyes. 'And you, Ariel, must go ter the North, ter unlock the power of Air and the gift of wisdom an' the mind.'

Ariel nodded her head up and down, all the time staring at Mrs Duggery with her huge eyes.

For a few seconds, they were silent. Everything in the big house was still.

Then Mrs Duggery said, 'If the stone shines with a blue

light, you're on the right path.'

As if to echo her words, it pulsed with a bright blue glow.

'And if we're not?' asked Flame.

'It'll change colour – watch it an' you'll know,' replied Mrs Duggery. She leaned forward. 'Now, remember – the key to your strength lies in the balance between the four a you. You mus' support each another, if one of you finds it too hard – but at the same time you mus' also focus on yer own power. You mus' never lose your own power in tryin' to help one another.'

She looked around at each of them in turn again. They watched her, silent, feeling the depth in her dark eyes.

'Do you all understand?'

'Yes,' they replied.

'Then put yer hands on the stone,' said Mrs Duggery. She held it out on her tiny, wrinkled palm. The four Sprite Sisters drew closer and stretched out their hands. Flame put her hand on top of Mrs Duggery's, then Marina, then Ash, then Ariel on the top.

A dazzling blue light burst out from the stone.

The four girls gasped – and then laughed and took their hands away. Mrs Duggery smiled. Grandma watched on, her face still and calm.

'Remember, the stone will help you – but you mus' learn ter guide yourselves,' said Mrs Duggery. 'Listen to the voice inside you.'

The Sprite Sisters each nodded.

'Now, keep this stone safe,' said Mrs Duggery, handing it to Ash. 'You will be its Keeper, as it comes from the Earth.'

'Thank you,' said Ash, holding the stone on her open palm. It glowed with a faint blue light – and then went out.

'Now, I think we'd better get on, Marilyn, or we'll never get this furniture sorted,' said Mrs Duggery.

The four Sprite Sisters hesitated. There were so many questions they wanted to ask the tiny old lady – but Mrs Duggery had done with talking.

'Go on now – get you off outside in the sunshine,' she said, swooshing the girls away with her hand.

The Sprite Sisters raced down the wide mahogany staircase, through the hallway, then the kitchen and burst out into the garden. They whooped and raced their way across the lawn to the big lime tree. There they swung on the black tyres that hung from the high branches. The summer holiday lay ahead and they felt free.

'It's all so *exciting*!' said Ariel.

Flame leaned back on the swing and looked up at the sunlight shimmering through a million leaves above her.

'We must not forget to go and mend another bit of the roof, later,' she murmured.

They were racing their bikes over the lawn, when Mum walked out of the house and called to Marina. 'Verena is on the phone and wants to say goodbye to you.'

Marina ran to the house and for the next twenty minutes talked to her friend – the friend she liked but could not trust. When she put the phone down, she felt relieved that Verena was going and that she and Flame would not need to fight any more.

Later, Quinn and Janey McIver cycled over with their tennis racquets. Flame and Janey played three sets of tennis against Quinn and Marina. Quinn and Marina just won.

Then Marina took Janey up to her room to listen to some music, while Quinn and Flame stretched out on the lawn under the beech tree and talked.

'This is just the most amazing place in the world,' said Quinn, with a dreamy look on his face.

Flame smiled and gazed into his dark eyes.

'And you are the most amazing girl,' he said, with a quick smile.

Flame's heart pounded as he moved closer to her on the grass. She was quite sure he was about to kiss her – her first ever kiss – when Ariel ran up and flopped down next to them.

Quinn laughed and Flame glared – then Mum called them in for tea. Quinn gave Ariel a piggyback to the house and Flame followed.

Hopeless, she thought. My romance will be forever doomed by my younger sisters.

As the Sprite family and the McIvers gathered around the tea table on the terrace at Sprite Towers, Glenda Glass drove Verena to London's Heathrow Airport. For most of the three-hour journey in the big silver car, Verena stared silently out of the window, thinking about her mother and father and how much she disliked her grandmother.

At the airport, Glenda went with her granddaughter to the check-in, then said a cool goodbye. Special flight attendants would look after the girl who was travelling alone to Buenos Aires.

As Glenda drove back up the motorway, she thought about her plans for the summer – and her immediate plans for Sprite Towers.

In his London office, Stephen Glass looked out of the window at a jet, high up in the sky, and phoned his daughter on her mobile as she waited for her flight. 'Take care, darling,' he said. 'Let me know when you've arrived safely.'

And in Buenos Aires, nearly seven thousand miles away, Zoe Glass, mother of Verena, estranged wife of Stephen and sister of Oswald Foffington-Plinker, waited anxiously for her daughter to arrive and wondered what lay ahead.

At Sprite Towers that night, Flame Sprite lay in bed and wondered what the future held.

The last image in her mind, before she fell asleep, was of Glenda Glass standing outside Sprite Towers in the moonlight.

CHAPTER THIRTEEN

✳

THE BATTLE FOR SPRITE TOWERS

✳ ✳

✳

WHEN SHE thought about it later, Flame felt she should have known something was about to happen. Several times during Saturday she had a flash of Glenda Glass in her mind, just as she had the night before.

And Grandma – she, too, felt uneasy all day. There was a strange feeling in the air.

After an early breakfast, Mum and Dad left in the big red car to attend the wedding of some friends. They would be away for the night and were not expected home until Sunday evening. Despite the horrible worry of the roof, they were happy.

Mum and Dad rarely went away together and they felt glad to be alone for the weekend. Their smart wedding clothes lay across the back seat of the car and their faces shone with excitement.

The Sprite Sisters and Grandma waved them off, as they pulled away down the long, leafy drive.

For most of the morning, Grandma weeded the Rose Garden, then went into bake bread and cakes.

The four girls did their chores, then spent much of the day with the magic stone. They carried it about all over the grounds and house – but nothing happened. It did not light up with even the faintest blue glow.

'Is there something the matter with it?' asked Ariel.

'I don't know,' replied Ash.

'I thought Mrs Duggery said it would light up when we are on the right path,' said Ariel.

'Well, we're either not on the right path or it doesn't work on Saturdays,' said Ash, staring at the brown-grey stone on her palm. She put it in her jeans pocket.

'Come on, let's go and play with the rabbits.'

The highlight of Flame's afternoon was when Quinn telephoned to say thank you for the game of tennis and tea.

'You go all soppy when you speak to him,' observed Ariel.

Flame tossed back her hair and flounced out of the room.

'What did I say?' said Ariel, as Grandma told her off.

And so they went on.

Later in the afternoon, Flame walked over the lawn. In the middle, she stopped and turned to look back up at Sprite Towers.

What is it, she wondered? There is something not right . . .

Grandma stood still in the kitchen, aware of a chilly feeling passing through her. There is something not right, she thought.

Otherwise, the day passed smoothly.

As the last quarter moon rose in the July sky, Flame, Marina, Ash and Ariel Sprite climbed into their beds. Downstairs, in the drawing room, Grandma sat on a big armchair watching a film. Bert was on her lap. She stroked his long silky ears.

The film had just that moment finished, when Bert raised his head and barked sharply.

He jumped off Grandma's lap and ran to the window.

'What is it, Bert?' she said, following him. She drew back the curtain and gazed out into the darkness. Bert growled a long low growl.

Grandma was suddenly aware of the pumping of her heart. What's happening, she thought.

Then she heard it – a deep, unearthly rumble.

As if from nowhere, the wind blew with an almighty gust. Suddenly, all she could hear was a roaring noise so loud that it drowned out Bert's barking.

Grandma's heart began to beat faster with fright. She

felt the whole house move and creak.

She peered out into the darkness. The trees down the long leafy drive were swaying so violently they looked as if they would snap.

Bert barked and barked. Close to the house, a tree branch cracked and fell to the ground, smashing into smithereens as it hit the gravel.

My God! thought Grandma terrified. *The roof! The chimneys might fall . . . I must get the girls down!*

She ran out of the drawing room and started to mount the stairs as the four Sprite Sisters came running down towards her.

'What's happening?' they all cried, as a huge crack came from the roof.

The lights flickered and a second later, there was a massive bang from outside the front of the house. Something big exploded on the ground.

Grandma and the four girls jumped, their faces white with terror, their hearts pounding. They huddled together on the stairs.

'It feels as if we are under attack!' cried Flame.

Hearing these words, Grandma stepped back from her granddaughters and looked up to the ceiling.

The lights flickered again.

'*What is it?*' cried the Sprite Sisters.

Then BANG! There was another loud crack from the roof and a thunderous crash. Whatever it was had also fallen to the ground.

Bert barked as hard as his small lungs would allow.

'This isn't a normal storm!' shouted Grandma above the din.

The four girls watched her, terrified.

'*The towers!*' shouted Grandma. '*The towers might fall!*'

Then Flame moved towards her, shouting: 'We must go down – *quickly! Come on!*'

She ran down the stairs, the others haring after her, as another loud crack came from the roof above them.

Ariel screamed.

Grandma shouted, '*Hurry!*'

'*Quick – in here!*' shouted Flame, thrusting open the door of the library. Marina, Ash and Ariel ran in and huddled together on the sofa.

Grandma ran to the desk, grabbed the telephone and punched in the emergency number. 'The line's dead!' she shouted, slamming it down.

She and Flame rushed to the window and stared out. Clouds whooshed across the clear night sky. The silver sliver of the moon shone bright.

And then they saw her.

Standing in moonlight, in the middle of the lawn with her arms stretched out wide, was Glenda Glass.

'Oh my God!' cried Flame.

Grandma stared – her mouth dropped open.

'*It's her!*' shouted Flame. '*We must do something! She is using her dark powers to hurt the house!'*

Marina, Ash and Ariel ran to the window – saw Glenda Glass and screamed in terror.

'Quick, girls!' shouted Grandma. *'There's no time to lose – use your powers! Use your powers to stop her!'*

Ariel clutched Grandma and sobbed. Ash was as white as a sheet. Marina felt like jelly. And Flame's mind raced.

'Come on, we must use our powers – NOW!' she yelled. 'Raise your hands and send your magic power against her! All of you!'

Ariel loosened her grip on her grandmother and walked slowly towards the window, whimpering. The house cracked and groaned.

'Come on, Ariel – HURRY!' cried Flame.

As the four girls lifted their hands and pointed their fingers towards Glenda Glass, there was another loud crack – this time from the corridor outside the library. The lights flickered again as Grandma walked quickly towards the door. High above her, a big atlas began to slide from its high shelf – then fell through the air.

Grandma cried out as it caught her on the side of her head. Then she fell to the ground.

'GRANDMA!' screamed the four Sprite Sisters, running to her across the room.

'Grandma!' cried Flame. 'Grandma! Can you hear me?'

Marilyn Sprite lay in a heap. Marina, Ash and Ariel began to cry.

Frantically groping for the side of Grandma's neck, Flame tried to feel her pulse. 'She's unconscious,' she said, her voice wavering. 'Turn her – we must turn her over!'

Quickly, they rolled Grandma on to her left side, then drew up her right leg slightly and raised her right arm.

The four girls stared at her, sobbing.

Suddenly, there was the most incredible cacophony – a banging, cracking, exploding noise, so loud it felt as if Sprite Towers had broken in two. The whole house shook as if in an earthquake. The two towers leaned and groaned. The glass blew out of one of the conservatory windows with a loud bang. Down by the stables, a large branch fell on one of the rabbit hutches and smashed through the roof.

And then the lights went out.

The four Sprite Sisters stood in complete darkness.

As the wind howled around the house, Flame stumbled back to the library window.

'*Leave Grandma for the moment!*' she shouted. '*We must stop Glenda!*'

Marina, Ash and Ariel fumbled their way towards her in the darkness.

'We've been focusing on Glenda, but we must focus on ourselves. We're strongest when we're balanced together,' shouted Flame. '*Hold hands!* Holds hands and make the Circle of Power!'

'We need to be in our positions!' shouted Marina,

moving towards the south-facing window.

In the darkness, the four shivering, terrified Sprite Sisters moved into a circle: Flame at the East, Marina at the South, Ash at the West and Ariel at the North.

Outside on the lawn, Glenda Glass laughed like a mad woman. She raised her hand and hurled another bolt of dark power at the roof.

I will soon have the Sprites out of there, she thought – but I must not damage the house too much. I must leave the magic intact.

The wind tore through the attics, it tore around the towers and it tore through the garden.

Tiles spun from the roof and crashed on the ground below. The huge house shook and let out an almighty roar. Ariel, Ash and Marina screamed.

'*Hold on – hold the power!*' shouted Flame, over the din.

The four Sprite Sisters clutched each others' hands as tight as they could.

'*Focus!*' shouted Flame. '*Focus your minds! Call in your power!*'

'Where's the stone?' shouted Marina.

Frantically, Ash groped in the pocket on her pyjama top.

'I've got it here!' she shouted, pulling it out.

'Put it in the centre of the circle!' yelled Marina.

Ash bent down and put the magic stone on the floor

between them, then stood up and took Marina and Ariel's hands once more.

Panting hard, Flame cried out, '*Fire!*'

Marina cried out, '*Water!*'

Ash shouted, '*Earth!*'

And little Ariel, her face streaked with tears, shouted, '*Air!*' in her loudest voice.

The magic stone began to glow. Blue light started to pulse through the circle of the Sprite Sisters' four inter-linked arms.

'Hold the power!' yelled Flame.

In the middle of the Circle, the blue light from the stone grew stronger and stronger – and so did the Sprite Sisters' power. Within seconds, in the blackened room and in the howling gale, the stone and the four Sprite Sisters became a dazzling ball of light.

'Close your eyes!' shouted Flame. 'Don't look – feel it!'

Outside, Glenda Glass's hands dropped like lead weights. Her knees sagged and she fell to the grass.

Without being touched by a single branch or falling tile, her body began to ache as it had never ached before. Huge bruises started to appear on her face and limbs. By the following morning, she would look as if she had fallen from a great height.

For some minutes, she lay groaning on the lawn. Then she pulled herself up and began to crawl over the grass on her hands and knees. By the side of the house, she managed to stand by pulling herself up on a tree.

For the next quarter of a mile, she hobbled very, very slowly to her car, which she had left at the bottom of the drive. It was a long, painful walk for Glenda Glass and one that she would never forget.

The instant that the power of the stone was released and fused with the Sprite Sisters' power, everything changed.

The clocks stopped. The wind dropped instantly. The clouds stopped moving across the night sky. Bert stopped barking. The house lights flickered on again and the Sprite Sisters found themselves standing in a circle, holding hands. Balance was restored.

'What happened?' whispered Ash, as if waking from a dream. She looked down and saw the magic stone – which was now its usual brown-grey colour – and picked it up from the floor.

On the other side of the library, Grandma groaned softly.

'What happened?' she asked, trying to sit up on the floor. 'Ow, my head hurts . . .'

The four Sprite Sisters ran across the room to help her on to the sofa. Then they fell on to the armchairs and sofa, exhausted.

For some while, the five of them sat, slumped, staring into space. Then Flame and Marina hauled up their weary bodies and went through to the kitchen. There, they heated a saucepan of milk and made five mugs of thick hot chocolate. Flame carried the tray of mugs through to the library. Marina brought a second tray with a large knife, five small plates and one of Grandma's special fruitcakes. She cut huge slices for them all, as Flame handed out the hot drinks.

'I'm ravenous,' said Ash, chomping her cake and swigging her hot chocolate.

'So am I!' said Ariel.

The hot drink and the fruitcake revived them all, but still no one felt able to talk.

After a while, Flame asked, 'How do you feel, Grandma?'

'A bit shaken – but all in one piece, thank you, dear.' She paused. 'And how are you all?'

Flame made a loud 'phew' sound and smiled at her grandmother. 'We're all okay – I think – but the house must be in a heck of a mess.'

Grandma looked around the room. 'A lot of books have fallen off the shelves.'

'We can soon put those back, Grandma,' said Flame. 'I am not sure how we will mend the rest. It sounded as if half the roof came in. It's a wonder the towers didn't fall.'

'Let's have a look out of the window,' suggested Grandma, pulling herself up, one hand on her head.

Marina and Ash took an arm each and led her to the window.

They all stood, gazing out. Even in the moonlight, they could see a scene of complete devastation.

'Oh, my word,' said Grandma, very softly.

'Whatever will we say to Mummy and Daddy?' whispered Ariel.

'Perhaps we should go and take a look round outside,' said Flame.

'No, dear, not tonight. Please don't.' Grandma sounded weary. 'Let's just all go to bed and get some rest. We will need all our energy tomorrow morning.'

'All right,' agreed Flame.

'Promise,' said Grandma, looking at her eldest granddaughter. 'Please don't start trying to sort this out tonight.'

'I promise, Grandma,' said Flame. 'Come on, let's get you up to bed.'

The Sprite Sisters and Grandma walked through the house. The paintings on the wall were wonky. Various pieces of china had smashed and lay in pieces on the floor. One of the windows on the big staircase, at the front of the house, had blown in. The glass lay scattered in fragments on the carpet.

At the bottom of the wide mahogany staircase, they stopped in front of the portrait of Sidney Sprite. It was the only painting in the hallway that had not tilted.

'Goodnight, Sidney,' they all said, as everyone in the Sprite family did, every night, when they went up to bed.

Then they climbed the stairs. That night, the girls saw their grandmother to bed first. They waited in her sitting room while she undressed, then helped her into her bed. When they were sure she was comfortable, they turned out the light and shut the door.

'Goodnight, Grandma,' they whispered.

'Do you think Grandma is all right?' said Marina, as they climbed the stairs to the second floor.

'I think so,' said Flame. 'How are you feeling?'

'Worn out,' replied Marina.

'It's a shame Mrs Duggery wasn't here to help us,' said Ash. 'She'd have stopped Glenda hurting the house.'

'Yes, where was Mrs Duggery when we needed her?' said Marina.

'I wonder why she didn't come? She must have known what was going to happen,' said Flame.

'How will we clear everything up before Mum and Dad get home – or explain it?' said Ash.

'I'm sure we'll think of something,' said Flame. Then she and Marina tucked their two younger sisters into bed.

'Is Glenda coming back again?' asked Ariel, clutching her teddy bear.

'No, pumpkin – she's gone. I can feel it,' said Marina.

The two older sisters left Ariel's bedroom and walked back along the corridor. Before they parted, they gave each other a big hug. Then they went to their bedrooms and slept like logs.

CHAPTER FOURTEEN

※

CHAOS

IT WAS not until ten o'clock on Sunday morning that the Sprite Sisters awoke. Rarely in their lives had they slept so late. Apart from Marina, who liked to lie in bed and read, the Sprites were a family who got going in the mornings.

Flame, Marina, Ash and Ariel pulled back their bedroom curtains, looked out of their windows – and gasped in horror.

The garden looked as if it had been through a hurricane. Huge branches, tiles and chimney pots lay scattered over the grass. The air was chill and the sky dull and heavy.

In haste, the Sprite Sisters pulled on their T-shirts and jeans and ran down to Grandma's room, where they found her dressed, though still a bit shaky.

Downstairs, Mrs Duggery had arrived and was cooking breakfast. The delicious smell of coffee, eggs, sausage and bacon, toast and honey wafted up the stairs as the girls raced down and burst into the kitchen.

'Mornin',' said Mrs Duggery, lifting fried eggs on to plates.

'We ought to start clearing up straightaway!' said Flame. 'We haven't got time for breakfast! Mum and Dad will be back at six!'

She ran towards the door to the garden.

'Eat yer breakfast first,' said Mrs Duggery, in a voice that would brook no nonsense.

Flame stopped by the door, her face tense.

'But haven't you seen the mess outside?' she protested. 'It's *chaos* out there!'

'All the more reason ter eat yer breakfast,' said Mrs Duggery, handing her a plate of food. 'How do you expect to do a full day's work on an empty stomach? Now, sit you down an' eat.'

Flame sighed heavily, took the plate of eggs and bacon and sat down at the table. 'Thank you,' she said, quietly.

Mrs Duggery turned to hand Grandma a plate of food and a cup of coffee.

'Mornin', Marilyn.'

'Morning, Violet – thank you.'

'How's the head feelin'?' said Mrs Duggery, looking Grandma up and down.

'Better, thank you,' Grandma smiled wanly.

The four Sprite Sisters and Grandma ate their breakfast, hungrily. Mrs Duggery watched them, holding a cup of tea in one hand and a chocolate biscuit in the other.

Nobody spoke.

Ariel looked at the tiny old lady with baleful eyes. Finally, in a quiet voice, she expressed what her sisters were thinking. 'Where *were* you last night, Mrs Duggery? Where were you when we needed you?'

Flame, Marina and Ash looked at Mrs Duggery with reproachful eyes.

'Why didn't you help us?' said Marina.

Flame didn't speak. Her face said it all.

Grandma was thoughtful.

Silence hung in the air.

Mrs Duggery met the Sprite Sisters' eyes with a level gaze.

The girls waited.

What Mrs Duggery said next would remain with them for the rest of their lives.

'You have ter learn to fight your own battles.'

'But we could have been *killed*!' said Ash, in a tremulous voice.

Mrs Duggery nodded, then said, 'I was watchin' more 'an you think.'

They were silent again.

Then Mrs Duggery said, 'You did well. You used the power stone, just as you were meant ter. You should be proud of yerselves.'

The spirits of the three younger girls rose, but Flame was not so easily convinced.

'Proud? The house is in *pieces*!' she cried. 'Have you seen the *mess* out there? What on *earth* shall we tell Mum and Dad?'

Mrs Duggery met Flame's glare with steely eyes.

'You have magic powers, don't yer?'

Flame was taken aback by the sharpness in her voice.

'Well?'

'Yes,' she nodded.

'Well, then *use* 'em,' said Mrs Duggery. 'Use your gifts – all a you. There's a lot ter do today, but if we work hard and use our powers, then all shall be well.'

For a few seconds, nobody spoke. There were so many things they wanted to know – but Mrs Duggery began dunking her biscuit in her tea, and it was clear she was done answering questions.

Then Grandma said in a clear, level voice, 'We've got about seven and a half hours, before Colin and Ottalie get home.'

'How can we mend the roof and clear up the garden in that time?' asked Marina, incredulous.

Grandma cast a quick look at Mrs Duggery, as if to say, '*Is* it possible?'

Mrs Duggery's eyes twinkled.

'You'll see,' she said, taking another chocolate biscuit.

Everybody sighed.

'Now eat up yer breakfast,' said Mrs Duggery. 'Don't rush. There's time enough.'

The Sprite Sisters' confidence rose. They munched their food and swigged their orange juice. For a while, all was quiet in the big kitchen.

Then the tiny lady in the lilac knitted hat said, 'I want you ter think about yer individual powers.'

The Sprite Sisters looked at her – and waited.

'Flame, you've the power to illuminate an' cleanse. Your power of Fire will be most useful in the garden.'

'Yes,' said Flame.

Mrs Duggery nodded, then turned to Marina. 'You also have the power ter cleanse – with water – and to put back the heart in ter the house.'

Marina nodded.

Ash watched Mrs Duggery, her face expectant. 'Heal the trees, bind the tiles an' the chimneys – anything that needs holdin' in place,' she said to the girl with soft brown eyes. 'Your power will allow you ter feel things that aren't visible to the eye. Work with Ariel, ter sense where the things are that need mendin'.'

She turned to the youngest Sprite Sister.

'Ariel, you'll lift things an' return 'em to their rightful place, then Ash will bind 'em.'

'Yes,' said the two younger Sprite Sisters together.

Mrs Duggery stood up. 'Right, well then if yer all ready, we best get started.'

The Sprite Sisters stood up and looked at Mrs Duggery.

'You won't forget this day,' she said.

And they didn't.

The Sprite Sisters would look back on that day as the day they learned to make the things that were broken in their life whole once again.

It was the day that they came into their power in a way they had never felt before.

It was a day when chaos turned to calm.

All day long, Mrs Duggery used her magic powers to mend the house. Somehow – though none of them saw her do this – she put back the glass in the shattered windows on the staircase and conservatory and mended the broken ornaments in the hallway.

In the garden, Flame used her power of Fire to incinerate all the branches that lay on the ground. As she lifted her hand and pointed her finger, huge pieces of wood were turned to fine ash, which blew away in the breeze. Bit by bit, the garden was cleared of debris.

In the house, Ariel used her magic power to replace all the books that had fallen in the library, then Ash bound them still, so they would not fall again. Then they went up to the attics, where they worked with Marina, to mend the roof from the inside. When this task was done, Marina used her magic to call in the power of the heart – and filled the rooms with warmth and light.

Using their power to sense where things needed attention, Ash and Ariel moved from room to room through the house and put things back in their rightful place. Marina followed. Bit by bit, room by room, Sprite Towers began to feel like home once again.

Grandma swept and tidied, aware that her fingers were tingling in a way she had not felt them tingle in forty years. She smiled as she looked at her long, slim dancer's hands.

Not all went happily, however.

Just as it looked as if things were finally mended and the garden clear, Flame ran into the kitchen with a white face.

Marina, Ash and Ariel had just come downstairs for a sandwich and were sitting at the table.

'What is it?' said Ash, alarmed.

'What's happened?' cried Ariel.

'You'd better come and have a look,' said Flame.

The four Sprite Sisters ran over the lawn. Grandma followed. Bert lolloped along behind, his big ears flapping.

Flame led them to the hutches by the stables.

There on the ground, laid out on a small bed of straw, was Ash's rabbit, Fudge. His little brown and white body was cold and stiff.

Ash and Ariel burst into tears.

'Oh no!' they cried. 'Poor Fudge!'

'I'm so sorry,' said Flame, wiping the tears from her face.

Ash bent down and stroked the rabbit's fur, tears pouring down her face. Ariel could not touch it and reached for her grandmother's arms.

'A branch came through the roof of the hutch,' explained Flame. 'I am sure he was killed instantly.'

Marina got down and stroked the little animal. 'He's so cold,' she said, sadly. 'To think that horrible woman *killed* our rabbit! I shall never forgive her!' And she, too, wept.

For some minutes, they stayed there. Then Ash stood up, wiped her teary eyes and said, 'We will bury him.'

Flame fetched a spade from the garden shed. Marina found two pieces of wood and bound them together with twine, in the shape of a cross. Ariel and Grandma picked a lovely bunch of wild flowers and put them in a jam jar of water. Ash made a bed of leaves, then carried her rabbit to the edge of the Wild Wood.

'He'll feel free here,' she said.

Then, Flame dug a hole in the ground, half a metre deep.

When this was done, Ash laid the little body of the rabbit into the hole. Flame dragged back the soil and covered the hole. Marina pushed the cross into the dark earth.

As the late afternoon sun broke through the clouds and shone down on the Wild Wood, they said some prayers. Ash hoped Fudge would feel happy and thanked him for being a nice pet.

Ariel wept. They all felt very sad.

Afterwards, Flame went to put back the spade, whilst the others made their way to the house.

Grandma put her arm around Ash's shoulders as they walked over the wide, rolling lawn.

'I still haven't used my power to bind the tree roots,' said Ash looking round, ever conscientious of the garden.

'Don't worry about that now, love,' said Grandma. 'You can do it tomorrow. They won't come to any harm tonight.'

'Do you think Glenda Glass may come back?' Ash looked up at her grandmother.

'No, I don't think she will be back,' Grandma said and squeezed Ash's hand.

'Look!' shouted Marina, pointing up to the roof. 'There's Mrs Duggery!'

They looked up and all burst out laughing.

There she was, the tiny old lady in the lilac knitted hat and big brown boots, clumping along the ridge tiles of Sprite Towers, high in the air! In her arms was a stack of pantiles.

'She's *amazing*!' said Marina. 'Those tiles are really heavy and she's carrying a whole pile of them!'

They shouted and waved to Mrs Duggery – who stopped for a moment and gave them a glinty-eyed smile.

'Come down and have a cup of tea and some chocolate biscuits!' shouted Grandma, as loud as she could through cupped hands, then beckoning with her hand.

From where they stood, it looked as if Mrs Duggery nodded.

'I'm sure the chocolate biscuits will do the trick!' laughed Flame, as she joined them.

'Look at the roof!' said Ash, her face full of wonder. 'It's all mended!'

The four Sprite Sisters and their grandmother stood, gazing up at the roof of Sprite Towers.

'Amazing,' said Grandma.

Then they turned around to look at the garden.

'No one would believe this place looked as if it had been hit by a hurricane a few hours ago!' said Marina.

Then they all went in for tea and biscuits.

CHAPTER FIFTEEN

SUNDAY EVENING AT SPRITE TOWERS

MUM AND Dad motored up the drive of Sprite Towers at half past five that afternoon, happy and relaxed. They'd had a lovely weekend away. The wedding had been fantastic. They had danced late into the night and seen a lot of old friends. Now, after a long drive back from one side of the country to the other, they were glad to be home.

'*Whatever's that?*' said Dad, with a start. He clutched the steering wheel and peered up at the roof of Sprite Towers.

'What?' said Mum.

'That!'

Mum stared at the big house, now looming in front of

her. 'What do you mean?'

'Mrs Duggery!'

'What about her?'

'*She's on the roof!*' Dad looked like a fish: his mouth was open wide.

'Blimey, are you feeling okay?' chortled Mum.

'No, she was! I saw her!'

'Well, I didn't,' said Mum, laughing loudly. 'And since it is *extremely* unlikely, in any circumstance that I could possibly think of – I have to say, Colin, that I think you are seeing things.'

Dad swung the car round on the gravel at the front of the house and braked hard.

'Are you sure you're okay?' Mum touched his shoulder.

Dad nodded.

'Why on earth should Mrs Duggery be on the roof?'

'I have no idea,' he replied. 'Forget it.' And he climbed out of the car.

The front door of Sprite Towers opened and out ran their four daughters, followed by Grandma and Bert.

'How was it, Daddy?' asked Ash.

'Wonderful, sweetheart!' he said, giving her a big hug.

Then he stopped and stared at the ground – and shook his head very quickly, as if it was all jumbled up.

'What's the matter?' asked Ash.

Mum laughed. 'Your father thought he saw Mrs Duggery on the roof! I think he's tired from the long drive!'

The Sprite Sisters stared at their mother in horror.

'Very strange,' said Dad. 'I could have sworn she was walking along the ridge tiles with a stack of pantiles in her arms . . .'

Ariel took his hand in hers and put on her serious face. 'Don't worry, Daddy, I've seen her up there, too.'

Alarm bells rang in the heads of Flame, Marina, Ash and Grandma.

'Sounds as if you had a good night out!' said Grandma, walking towards her son and hugging him.

'Hello, Ma,' he said, putting an arm around her shoulders. 'How are you? I hope this lot haven't worn you out.'

'No, they've been fine,' she smiled. 'We've had an interesting time.'

She said the word 'interesting' very deliberately. The four Sprite Sisters threw each other an amused look.

'Oh – what have you been up to?' asked Dad.

'Ash's rabbit, Fudge, was killed,' said Ariel, quickly.

'Killed? What happened? Did a fox get him?'

'No, Dad,' Ash pushed past Ariel. 'He just died.'

'Oh dear – poor old Fudge.' Dad looked sad.

'We buried him at the edge of the Wild Wood,' said Marina.

'That's a good place,' said Dad.

'I expect you'd both like a cup of tea,' said Grandma. 'Let's go in.'

Mum and Dad walked in through the front door,

through the hall and into the kitchen.

Everything looked as it should. The house was tidy. The garden looked wonderful. Bert looked pleased to see them. Their daughters looked radiant and Grandma smiled happily.

Twenty minutes later, they all sat down to high tea on the terrace. The late afternoon sun shone as they munched sandwiches, freshly baked scones dripping with home-made strawberry jam, plates of fresh raspberries and cream and huge pieces of chocolate cake.

Grandma poured China tea from a big silver teapot.

Mrs Duggery joined them and ate an enormous piece of chocolate cake. Her eyes shone as she swallowed it down.

'You make wonderful cake, Marilyn,' she said, between mouthfuls.

'Thank you,' said Grandma. 'I do enjoy cooking.'

'Just as well with this lot to feed,' chortled Dad.

'And just as well that you and Ash love growing vegetables and fruit,' added Mum. She sat back in her chair and looked out at the huge garden. 'It is wonderful here.'

'Ah yes – I have some very good news!' announced Dad.

Mum turned to smile at him. He looked back at her lovingly.

'You mother and I have worked it out,' he said.

'What?' asked the Sprite Sisters.

Dad caught Grandma's eye – and noticed the look of relief on her face.

'What's happened?' the girls clamoured.

'I got offered a terrific contract – that's what!' said Dad, triumphantly. 'I met a chap at the wedding – Stephen Glass knew him and recommended me. The man asked me if I'd be interested in working on a new scheme in the centre of the city. It's a big job and will last several years.'

'That's fantastic, Dad!' they all shouted.

He looked again at Grandma. 'What it means . . . what it means is, that your mother and I can say no to Oswald's offer. It means that, if we are careful, we shall have enough money to repair the roof.'

'Oh, that's *wonderful!*' exclaimed Marina.

'So you mean we can stay at Sprite Towers?' asked Ariel, in her breathy voice.

'Yes, love – that's exactly what I mean.'

There was much whooping and delight at this news. The girls even hugged Mrs Duggery, though she was still eating her chocolate cake.

When the telephone rang a little later and Dad went to answer it, he was confidently able to say, 'Thank you, but no – and I *mean* no,' to Oswald Foffington-Plinker at the other end of the line.

He heard Oswald sigh heavily, drooping at the other end of the telephone line. He knew that Glenda Glass would not be pleased and Oswald would cop it.

'Did Verena get to Buenos Aires safely?' Dad asked, quickly.

'Yes, thank you,' spluttered Oswald.

'Let's hope Zoe comes home soon. You must be concerned about your sister.'

'Yes, I hope so, too, Colin,' said Oswald. 'Lord knows what Zoe's doing out there.'

'And Glenda? Where is she?' asked Dad.

'She's about to leave for a long holiday – doesn't look at all well. She's covered in bruises – says she had a nasty fall.'

'Oh dear – well, I hope she soon recovers,' said Dad, politely. Then he added, 'Sounds as if you could both do with some relaxation.'

'Yes,' replied Oswald, wryly. 'Certainly could, old chap.'

'So, Oswald – that's enough about buying Sprite Towers. Let's leave it there, shall we?'

'Okay, old chap,' agreed Oswald.

Dad walked out on to the terrace punching the air.

Everyone else (except for Mrs Duggery, who only gave twinkly smiles occasionally), burst out laughing.

'Oswald has agreed to drop the offer and stop hassling us,' said Dad, sitting down again.

'Oh, thank goodness for that!' exclaimed Mum.

'And Glenda Glass has gone away for a long holiday,' continued Dad, looking at Mum and Grandma with a meaningful expression.

'Oh,' responded Mum. 'Well . . . that's . . . good.'

'Oswald said she'd had a bad fall.'

The Sprite Sisters tried to keep straight faces.

'Serves her right,' muttered Ash, under her breath.

'She's an evil old hag,' said Marina.

'Oh?' said Mum, turning to look at her. 'That's not a very nice way to describe someone.'

'Well, sometimes it's the only way.' Marina crossed her arms over her chest and looked resolute.

Mum pursed her lips and said, 'Hmm, I know what you mean.'

Mrs Duggery licked her lips and swallowed her final mouthful of chocolate cake. Then she took a big swig of tea and stood up.

'Right, well I'm orf now,' she said.

Mum looked surprised and stood up. 'Okay – well, thank you for your help, Mrs Duggery. We'll see you in the morning then.'

'No, I's orf now.'

Mum blinked. 'Oh, er, right . . . Well – thank you again.'

Mum looked at Grandma, who shrugged as if to say, 'That's the way it is.'

The Sprite Sisters ran to get their bicycles.

Outside the front door, Mum and Dad shook Mrs Duggery's hand. Grandma gave her a big hug.

'Thank you so much, Violet,' she smiled.

The old lady's eyes gleamed. 'You're very welcome, my dear. You take care now.'

Flame felt her heart pounding. She's going, she thought

– Mrs Duggery is leaving us. She stepped forward and bent down to hug her. 'Thank you – for everything.'

Mrs Duggery leaned closer to Flame and said gruffly into her ear, 'The sign of the crossed circle. Thas what yer need to look for.'

Then Marina came forward and hugged her, too – as did Ash and Ariel.

Mrs Duggery stood back and looked at them, her eyes still gleaming. Her face seemed to say, 'You'll do well.'

Then the tiny old lady in the lilac knitted hat climbed on to her old boneshaker bicycle and started to pedal very slowly down the middle of the drive.

Mum, Dad and Grandma waved.

The four Sprite Sisters got on their bicycles and cycled beside Mrs Duggery: Flame and Ariel one side, Marina and Ash the other, like outriders proudly guarding something very precious.

Together, they cycled down the long leafy drive.

At the gates of Sprite Towers, the Sprite Sisters stopped and got off their bicycles.

Mrs Duggery kept on riding, her tiny feet pushing down on the huge pedals.

The girls stood, silently watching, as she cycled off down the lane.

'Where does she go to?' asked Ash.

'Heaven knows,' said Flame. Half of her wanted to get on her bike and follow the tiny old lady in the lilac knitted hat, and the other half knew that she had to let her go.

'Will we ever see her again, do you think?' asked Ariel.

'I don't know,' replied Flame.

The four sisters watched as Mrs Duggery got smaller and smaller. Finally, she disappeared around the bend – and was gone.

They were silent.

Then Marina spoke up. 'What did she say to you, Flame?'

'*Look for the sign of the crossed circle,*' Flame replied.

Ash reached into her pocket and drew out the magic stone. 'What, like the markings on this?' she said.

Flame glanced at the stone, then turned her eyes again to the bend around which Mrs Duggery had disappeared.

For a moment, each of the Sprite Sisters stood still, deep in thought.

'Right – well we'd better get going then!' said Ariel, turning her bike. 'Race you home!'

And the four Sprite Sisters – the intense, tall girl with copper-coloured hair; the warm-hearted dark-haired girl with bright blue eyes; the earthy girl with brown hair and soft brown eyes and the naughty little blond one – leaned down on their handlebars and cycled, as fast as they could, back up the leafy drive, the warm evening light glowing on their faces.

Special Thanks

Big thanks to all the Piccadilly Press team for their skill, effort and enthusiasm, especially Brenda Gardner, Anne Clark, Mary Byrne, Melissa Patey and Margot Edwards. Also to Chris Winn for bringing the Sprite world to life in his illustration and to Anna Gould and Simon Davis for the striking cover.

Thanks, too, to Mike Butler and Sue Morgan at Jarrold's for the terrific launch, and to Sarah Skinner at Waterstone's for her support.

Thanks to my whizz new agents, Veronique Baxter and Georgina Ruffhead at David Higham Associates, and to Gina Pollinger for the introduction.

Thank you to all my wonderful friends for their kindness, particularly: David Brittain, Charlotte & Henry Crawley, Elisabeth & David Hawkey, Raffaele Zuppardi, Dinah John, Graham Woodford, Vern Freeman and Joanna Storey.

A big thank you to my parents, Alan & Janet Ebbage, to my son, Alex, and his partner, Hilary, and to my daughter, Rosie, for all their love and support.

Lastly, a huge thank you to the Sprite Sister fans – especially Marina Ebbage, Ava Kennedy, Lottie Houldey, Millie Nastali, Ayesha Marchant and Luisa Zuppardi.
Keep Spriting!